Go Fetch!

Look for these titles by
Shelly Laurenston

Now Available:

Pack Challenge
Here Kitty, Kitty

Go Fetch!

Shelly Laurenston

A Samhain publishing, Ltd. publication.

Samhain Publishing, Ltd.
577 Mulberry Street, Suite 1520
Macon, GA 31201
www.samhainpublishing.com

Go Fetch!
Copyright © 2009 by Shelly Laurenston
Print ISBN: 978-1-59998-633-3
Digital ISBN: 1-59998-141-6

Editing by Angela James
Cover by Scott Carpenter

First Samhain Publishing, Ltd. electronic publication: March 2007
First Samhain Publishing, Ltd. print publication: February 2009

Dedication

To all the Mikis in the world...you know who you are. And no, you can't hide.

And to my California family for taking such amazing care of me when I need it most.

Prologue

He sniffed the air again. He knew that smell dammit. He knew it from somewhere and it was going to drive him crazy until he remembered where. He kept moving, tracking the scent through the forest, as the rave went on in the clearing behind him.

He tore through the trees, the branches ripping at his fur. The scent shifted, so he stopped and spun, sniffed the air again and moved. This time he overshot, and they came out of the dark, attacking him from behind. Teeth sunk into his flank. Snarling and turning, he knocked them off before they could get a firm hold. One of his Pack mates and a full-blood joined him, but by the time the wolves turned, they were gone. His Pack mate spun in circles trying to see where they went, what they looked like, and who the hell they were.

They weren't Pride, they weren't wolf, and they sure as hell weren't human. Whatever they were, they didn't belong. They were out of their territory. He just wished he could remember where he'd smelled that scent before. He had no idea what had attacked him, but they were gone now. Their scent lingering, but still unknown.

Conall headed back to where he left his clothes. He'd protected the Pack, now he was ready to get back and enjoy the rave. He realized that, although his Pack mate had gone off to check the area more fully, the full-blood was following him. He let him, because he didn't fear him. The full-bloods let them into their territory because they knew they were there to protect a woman. His Alpha's mate—Sara.

Full-blood wolves howled and the full-blood with him stopped to join in. Conall let the sound wash over him. He loved that sound, more than anything. He stopped in his tracks and, without thought, leaned his head back and released a howl that blended in with the howls of the two hybrid Packs at the rave. This was something that didn't happen every day. Three Packs howling as one. All for one female. Sara deserved it, though. The female kicked major ass.

Another scent hit him. A scent he'd been coming to love lately. If she let him, he would roll in it all day. He headed toward that wonderful scent, happily realizing she was near his clothes.

He silently moved toward her. She sat on a rock, reading an oversized paperback book. Squinting, forced to use the moonlight and the light from the rave to illuminate whatever she read.

Up to this point, he hadn't been able to dedicate any real time to his pursuit of her—too busy trying to protect his Pack. The few times he'd approached her, she'd been less than receptive. A nice way of saying every time Conall came near her, she ran like a rabid pit bull was on her ass.

But now that they'd wiped out the Withell Pride—the Pack's sworn enemy—his time was his own. At least for the moment. So he could give her his full attention. Besides, she looked hot and, for once, she was on her own.

He padded up to her, her scent pulling on him like a leash, so close to her that his nose was just inches from her neck.

Like a flash, her upper body twisted, a good-sized hunting

knife in her hand. He shifted and blocked her arm with his. Good thing, too. She could have cut his throat from ear to ear with that thing.

Her eyes widened at the sight of him. Then she glanced down and her eyes widened even more. "What is it with you people and being naked?"

He loved how annoyed she sounded. "It's a shifter thing."

"That's fascinating, but if you don't put some clothes on I'm going to have to start chopping at things that are protruding." And he knew she would.

"My clothes are over there."

"Get 'em."

She lowered her arm and slipped the blade back into the sheath at her side. Conall had no doubt she knew how to use that knife. He'd seen her in action. She was an amazing hunter—for a human.

And an even more brilliant piece of ass.

Conall walked over to the pile of clothes he'd left by a tree and put them on as Miki went out of her way not to look at him. He'd seen the woman blow the head off a Pride female with a single rifle shot from a moving vehicle, but his cock seemed to unravel her. *Weird girl.*

He figured he'd have to say something since she was going out of her way not to speak to him. "I'm Conall…" he began.

"We already had this conversation."

"…Víga-Feilan," he finished. Just like that, she cut him off. That was new. Women never cut him off before. They didn't necessarily find him fascinating but they faked it real well. At least until they got laid.

But his last name did seem to interest her, even though she didn't look away from her book. "Víga-Feilan?" People always said his last name back to him. Like an echo. It was an odd name and one he wouldn't change for the world. "Isn't that Viking?"

He stared at her, his Harley T-shirt in his hands. "How the hell did you know that?" True, it was actually a Norse byname, but Viking was close enough. No one ever knew that. *Ever.* Miki was the first to call it right. Christ, he wanted her.

"There are these fascinating places with books in them. They're called libraries. When you're not chasing your tail or balancing a ball on your nose, you should think about going to one."

He watched the sly smile she had on those gorgeous lips and he grinned. Oh, yeah. He liked her more and more every second. A girl this mean would definitely be one hell of a wild ride.

Miki glanced up at his silence and raised an eyebrow at his smile. "You know, when you've got folks out there howling and sniffing my ass, I'd say it's kind of dumb to stand around staring at me. I might snap at any moment."

Christ, he loved her voice. Kind of low and husky, with that sweet Texas accent. It played right across his nerve endings. And he *had* sniffed her ass, but only once. "That sounds promising."

She sighed and went back to her book.

He finished getting into his clothes and then sat down in the dirt to pull his black Harley-Davidson boots on.

"What are you reading?" He didn't really care. He just wanted to hear her say something else.

"A book on wolves."

That did pique his interest. "Really?"

"Yeah. Will it be necessary for Zach and Sara to have sex in front of you?"

Conall's head snapped up at her sudden—and scary—change of topic. She stared straight at him and he realized she was serious. "What? No!"

"Are you sure? Because according to this, the Alphas are the only ones who can mate and they have to do it in front of the Pack."

"But we're human...sort of."

"But you run around in a Pack. So don't you do other Pack-like things?"

"Well...uh...I...that is, we..." Conall shook his head. "They will not be having sex in front of us. And trust me, we can all have sex."

Her eyes narrowed. "I see." She went back to her book.

Conall finished lacing up one boot and moved to the other. "So, Miki, what do you...?"

"I'm reading."

"...do?" He blinked. He'd never gotten dismissed so easily. And this girl was dismissing him all over the place. His annoyance peeked out, his voice heavy with sarcasm. "You're reading at a rave? You really know how to party, don'tcha?"

Without even looking up from her book, she gave him the finger.

Man, she is so mean. He was glad he had his jeans on. He was hard as a rock.

With his laces finished, he sat back and watched her. He marveled at how beautiful she was. Soft brown skin, the cutest dimples known to man, curly black hair framing that gorgeous face, and the tightest ass he'd ever seen.

She seemed to sense him watching her again. She looked at him and glared. "What now?"

"Just looking at you."

"Don't."

"Are you shy?" He didn't mind shy. He could learn to like shy. Hell, for one night of hot meaningless sex he could learn to like almost anything.

"In what sense?"

What the hell kind of question was that? "What?"

"In what sense are you asking am I shy? There are different types of shy. There are those who are shy of people. Those who are shy of animals—which you do qualify. And those who are only shy in certain situations. So which shy are you asking me about?"

"I have no idea now."

"Typical."

Okay, cute wasn't working with this one. He'd have to try something else. He was desperate. They were leaving the next day, and he wanted his last night in this dinky town spent between those thighs.

"You know, if you left the rave because you're nervous, I can take you home." Get her home. Get her settled. Get her wet. Then get her in bed. Yeah, that worked as a plan.

She turned to stare at him, her eyes shrewdly looking him over. "Is that a fact?"

Conall gave one of his patented innocent shrugs. He'd worked long and hard on being the big, nonthreatening guy. The guy women turned to for safety. No one ever knew that just below his flesh, he had chained one of the most dangerous wolves known to the Norse gods. A wolf descended from Loki himself. A wolf always fighting to let itself out. But Conall fought just as hard not to be like the rest of his family. So he'd chained the wolf. Almost like some people chain dogs to a spike in their backyard. He chained it and left it there. It only came out during the hunt or during a battle. But when he was human, it stayed chained and locked safely away where it could do no harm. A few bad experiences had already shown him no female, human or wolf, could handle the deadly wolf he had buried inside. No female brave enough to face that part of him.

He slowly stood up, watching her gaze travel his body as he moved. He put his hands in his pockets and lowered his eyes to give her what one woman termed the "sweetest, most innocent look" she'd ever seen seconds before she'd given him a killer blowjob. A look that had worked on many, many women before Miki. It would work now. "Sure, Mik. It's no problem."

She stared at him for a full minute before she burst out laughing. "You are so full of shit!"

Conall frowned and his body tensed. "Excuse me?"

"You heard me. You think I buy into this innocent act of yours? 'Oh, sweet Conall. He's just a big ol' teddy bear.'" She shook her head. "Teddy bear, my ass."

Conall was shocked. For the first time in a long time, a woman had shocked him. "You're serious?"

"Dead serious." She marked the page in her book with a leaf, stood, and walked to him. She tilted her head back so that she could see him clearly. "I've known you less than a week and I already see you, Conall. And you're nobody's teddy bear. I don't care what line of crap you try and sell everybody else." She studied him closely and he couldn't stop looking into those brown eyes of hers. She still had a bruise from where one of the Pride males slugged her when she tried to protect Sara. He'd snapped that fucker's neck himself.

"I see it in your eyes," she continued. "You're all wolf. But there's something more. Something..." She stared up at him and it felt like she was walking around his backyard, examining

15

his chained wolf, and he wasn't sure how he felt about that. Actually, he thought he'd locked that gate.

She nodded. "You're more like your name. A Viking. But you know what, Viking? I'm not some British Isle for you to conquer. So go find yourself some nice, wafer-thin girl who'll happily buy your bullshit. Whose heart you can break without a second thought. I'm off limits."

She stepped away from him but he couldn't stop staring at her. He'd never wanted anyone more in his life. Suddenly one night between those thighs didn't seem nearly enough.

"Miki?"

She looked at him, a small smile sliding across her beautiful lips. She was enjoying herself. "Conall?"

He stepped up to her and was impressed she didn't back away. "I just wanted to tell you something."

"Oh, yeah? What exactly?"

"That you're absolutely right."

"Am I now?"

"Yeah." Conall slid his hand behind the back of her neck and leaned down so their faces were close. "I ain't no teddy bear."

He snatched her to him, lifting her completely off the ground. Then he kissed her. The kind of kiss he'd wanted to give her since he first saw her. A raw, brutal kiss that, to his surprise, she returned. Her mouth opened and his tongue slipped in past her lips. She gave a moan that felt like nails ripping across the flesh on his back and made him so hard his cock hurt. His hands on her waist held her flat against him. He made sure his erection pressed into her as his tongue stroked hers, and he felt her warm hand through his T-shirt. But when her fingers clutched the fabric, trying to pull him even closer, he knew he had to have this woman.

He finally released her, lowering her back to the ground, but he kept his hand possessively on the nape of her neck and his forehead pressed against hers. He had to bend down to reach her, but he didn't care. Especially when all he wanted to do was rip her clothes off, flip her on her stomach, and mount her. He wanted to fuck her until they both screamed.

"Take me home, Miki." He was so desperate for her he could barely see.

She was panting, and if her heart were to beat any faster it would come out of her chest. He knew she wanted him. He could smell it.

Miki pulled her head back and looked him in the eye. She smiled. Not a forced one he'd seen her give others, but a real smile—warm and all his.

"Not on your life." She pulled herself from his arms and headed back to the rave without a backward glance. "Goodbye, Viking. Have a good life."

His cock was rock hard and he could still feel every place she'd touched him. He stood up to his full height and fought the urge to snatch her out of the rave and back to the closest hotel.

He heard a low growl and turned to see the full-blood wolf in a copse of trees nearby. He, too, watched Miki.

"Back off," Conall growled, causing the beta wolf to slowly back away. He returned his gaze to that fine ass moving through the crowd. He grinned as his canines extended. "This one's mine."

Chapter One

Six months later...

Miki's eyes snapped open and she realized she already had her hand around the shotgun she kept against her nightstand. She sat up, the gun still in her grasp. She had to shake her head to bring herself back to this reality. Miki didn't sleep. Not much anyway. But on those few times she actually did get some sleep, it was a helluva thing to actually wake her up. Especially lately. She'd been having these intense dreams... She shook her head again. She couldn't go down that road right now. She needed to focus.

She could hear crunching sounds coming from the front of her house. Well, Sara's house really. She'd rented it to Miki for practically nothing.

Miki slid out of bed in her T-shirt and sweatpants and steadied the weapon in both hands. She silently slipped from room to room, checking every corner as she went. Finally, she arrived at the front door. Taking a deep breath, she snatched it open and aimed.

"Howdy, Miki."

Miki lowered her gun. "Dammit, Eddie! What the hell are you doing here?"

Deputy Eddie Fogle continued to eat his chocolate-covered peanuts and seemed oblivious to the fact Miki was damn good and ready to blow his head off. "Just watchin' out for ya, darlin'." Smooth-talking bastard. The man leaned back against her porch railing, his incredibly long legs stretched out in front of him. She briefly wondered if he had to have his cowboy boots specially made. His feet were enormous.

"Did Marrec send you here?" Marrec had become like a mother hen since they'd kicked Pride ass six months ago, constantly checking up on Miki and Angelina. Not that she didn't appreciate it, but having a sheriff's deputy sitting out on her front stoop in the middle of the night seemed a little excessive.

"We just want you to be safe."

"Well, that's sweet and all—"

"You know, Miki," he cut in smoothly, "I'm so glad you're getting out of town for a bit. You deserve it. But I hope you won't be involving yourself with those Seattle-city folk like before. I'd really hate it if you upset Sara and Angelina or shame everybody in town. Again."

Miki shut her eyes in exasperation. Boy, Feds drag you out of Advanced Trig in handcuffs just once and some people never let you forget it. Besides, hadn't she already paid her debt to society? And exactly how long had the man been out here? She'd talked to her buddy Craig over five hours ago. They'd planned on meeting at a bar when she hit town and, depending on her mood, maybe going to one of Craig's infamous house parties. Craig had hinted at maybe getting back into the Game, but she'd told him no flat out. Damn wolves with their damn wolf hearing. Well, it didn't matter. Her days of risking federal prison were long over. She had bigger plans. So it didn't really matter what Fogle heard.

"My only plans are to help my friend celebrate her twenty-ninth and to become Doctor Kendrick, PhD."

"Good. Good. That's really nice to hear."

Miki watched him for several moments, then sighed. "You're not going anywhere, are you?"

"Not tonight. No. Some strange activity in town. Odd smells I'm not real comfortable with. But if it makes you feel better, we're also watching Angelina's house."

"It doesn't," she responded flatly.

Eddie chuckled. "When you see Sara, could you give her my love?"

"Of course."

"I sure do hope those Magnus boys are being good to her. Not sure about that Zach Sheridan fella." Miki fought the urge to roll her eyes. They'd all babied Sara. Of course, she now knew why. Sara had been one of them. Not of their Pack but a shapeshifter like, it turned out, most of her town. Apparently, Miki and Angelina were two of the few nonshifting humans within a one-hundred-mile radius. "And we sure do miss her 'round here."

"Yeah. Me, too."

"Then I guess it's about time you got that pretty little ass of yours over there, huh?"

"I haven't been avoiding her, Fogle. I've been working on my dissertation. And she understands that." They were all like a bunch of old women. Chastising her. She could practically see them shaking their collective paw at her.

"I didn't think you were avoiding Sara—maybe that other fella, though."

"Who? Zach?" She snorted. "I'd rip his balls off and wear them as a necklace."

"Nah, not him. The other one. That big fella. Conall, I think his name is."

"Oh give me a fuckin' break."

"Uh-huh." Eddie looked back at her with those wolf eyes that reflected light just like a dog's. "Did you know you moan Conall's name in your sleep?"

The man couldn't have startled her more if he'd punched her in the stomach.

She didn't have an answer, so she stepped back into her house and slammed the door. It didn't help she could hear his laughter through the thick wood.

She put her free hand to her face to rub her eyes in exasperation, but she smelled her scent on her fingers again. Dammit. Masturbating in her sleep again. Masturbating to Conall.

Well, this is spiraling out of control.

ᏸ

Conall Víga-Feilan, direct descendent of the Viking Overlord Sven Víga-Feilan and the Víga-Feilan Pack, dropped face down onto his bed. He was still wet from his third cold shower of the night. *Well, this is spiraling out of control.* How could one woman completely dominate his thoughts for six freakin' months? He hadn't masturbated this much since junior high.

But, Miki wasn't just some woman. She was the meanest woman he knew. And her meanness talked to him on a level he'd never experienced before. She brought out the wolf in him, which he'd learned to control a long time ago. But just thinking about her made his cock hard and his canines grow.

His whole life he'd had to accept the fact he wasn't like the other Víga-Feilans. His father had been too nice. Loved his Irish female too much. His uncle and grandfather had made his father's life a living hell while he lived with the Víga-Feilan Pack. It wasn't until he met Bruce Morrighan that everything changed. Bruce introduced Conall's father to the Magnus Pack. They had a lot of members and they were always looking for new ones. Jarl Víga-Feilan took his wife and newborn son and left the Víga-Feilan Pack for good. Since then, the Pack had been trying their best to get Conall to return to the fold. To become one of them. His cousin, Einarr, was especially determined to see him return. But there was no way he'd leave the Pack. Especially not now.

And not because the Pack needed him during this time of war. Or that Pack life really rocked with Zach and Sara in charge. He wasn't leaving because Sara's best friend was the woman of his dreams. A mean, sassy Texan with the sweetest smile he'd ever seen on a woman. He loved that smile. Loved to think about what that beautiful mouth could do to him.

Conall growled. Wrong thought. He shouldn't have gone there. He stood and headed back to his shower when a knock on his door stopped him.

"Yeah?"

Jake stuck his head in. "I smelled something on our property. But it wasn't Pride."

Conall frowned. "Are you sure?"

"It was different. But nothing I recognized."

Conall groaned. That had to be the same damn scent from the night of the rave. The scent he couldn't remember for the life of him. The whole thing was making him insane.

"Anybody else up?"

"Jim and Kelly."

"Get 'em. Bring 'em out with you. Kill anything that isn't one of us."

"You got it."

"And Jake? Don't hit on Kelly. She'll crush your windpipe and suck the marrow from your bones."

Jake looked so disappointed Conall almost felt bad for him. But not really.

Once Jake was gone, Conall stood in the middle of his bedroom wondering why he was standing in the middle of his bedroom. Then he remembered Miki. Well, Miki and oral sex. With a sigh, he started off again to the bathroom.

Zach was going to kill him when the water bill came.

Chapter Two

"So is Conall picking you up at the airport?"

Miki's hands balled into fists over her keyboard and her teeth clenched together. How many times were Sara and Angelina going to mention that man? It was bad enough she couldn't forget him. Bad enough she was jacking off to him in her sleep. The hardest thing she'd ever had to do was walk away from him that night at the rave. But she knew what guys like him could do. Guys with innocent smiles and all the right words. They came into your life, turned it completely upside down, and then left you. Alone, pregnant and bitter. At least that was how it had worked for her mother.

"If you mention that motherfucker one more goddamn time I am going to kick your ass all over this fuckin' airport."

Angelina calmly stared at her over her sour apple martini. "Hmm. Those sound like the tense cuss words of a woman that needs to get laid."

Miki snarled. She seemed to do that a lot around Angelina these days. Mostly because she wouldn't stop mentioning "sweet, adorable Conall".

How anyone could think that man was sweet was beyond her. Not with those eyes of his. Those beautiful blue eyes were anything but innocent. The man was a marauder. A conqueror. And he was looking at Miki like unclaimed territory in ancient

China.

"We're not having this discussion again."

"Okay. Fine." Angelina was silent. For about fifteen seconds. "But you do know that a vibrator can't really be your boyfriend."

Miki dropped her head into her hands. "I will not discuss Mr. Happy with the likes of you."

Angelina sighed. "I find the fact that you named your vibrator disturbing on so many levels."

"Best relationship I've ever had."

Angelina sipped her martini and eyed Miki over her glass. Miki picked up her Shirley Temple and stared back.

"I didn't know insanity ran in your family, Kendrick."

"We got it from yours, Santiago."

Angelina crossed her legs and Miki immediately looked around to watch the men watch Angie. Remarkable. The woman had the ability to distract every man in the room and she never seemed to notice. Or care.

"So, did you talk to Sara today?"

Relieved Angelina decided to back off the Conall discussion and not wanting to hit a beautiful woman in the face with her laptop computer, Miki answered, "Like four times. You'd think I wouldn't be seeing her in a few hours."

"I don't know why you're going to her house first. Why aren't you flying straight to Seattle?"

"Sara booked the tickets. She arranged this little stopover. I guess she misses me."

"Well, you'll like her place. It's nice. Just needs a porch."

Angelina had already been to Sara's new home in Northern California. Miki hadn't gone, instead opting to stay in Texas and plow through her thesis rewrites. She knew Sara understood, but she also knew Sara had been hurt. She missed her two friends, almost as much as they missed her.

"Whatever. At least I'll have a place to relax before I head up to Seattle. I'm already so stressed about all this shit. I keep rereading my notes and analyzing my thesis."

"And writing lists." Angelina gave her a warm smile. "Don't worry, Mik. You're going to be great."

"And what if I blow it, Angie?"

"What if you do? So? The world won't end."

Close enough. She had her whole future riding on this. Angie would never understand. Everything always came so easy to her. And Sara, being the canine that she was, never really asked for much. Miki, however, was being left behind and she knew it.

But not anymore. An assistant professor position at the university was hers once her dissertation was completed. She simply had to make sure she didn't blow it. The fact they wanted her at all still amazed her. She and her Seattle friends were infamous. Not only in the university where she got her undergrad and graduate degrees. But in schools across the country. From the time she dumped her clothes on the dorm room floor her freshman year, she'd been up to all sorts of hijinks and shenanigans.

Surprising to many, Miki only got busted once. In high school. The judge could have sent her off to juvenile detention or even tried her as an adult, but her mother had died the year before and the entire town turned out to make a plea on her behalf. Sara had even shown up using crutches. She'd never used crutches before in all the years Miki had known her up to that point. But there she stood in front of the judge, making a tearful plea for Miki while leaning on her pitiful crutches. It was quite the display and Miki would have laughed her ass off if she hadn't been scared to death she was going to prison.

In the end, she got one year of house arrest and three years of no computer or phone use. You would think that would have been enough to get her to keep the hijinks to a minimum once she got to college. Yet when you're eighteen, you always think you're untouchable. And for some unknown reason, she had been. The Feds couldn't find anything to nail her with and they'd tried. Then Miki disappeared. Okay, not really. She just went home. She had only begun working on her graduate degree when her grandmother became ill. At twenty-one she had no idea what the hell she wanted to do with the rest of her life anyway and could easily finish her degree long distance. She thought a year home would help.

But it was eight years and two master's degrees later and Miki was still trying to figure out what the hell she was going to do with her life.

"Trust me," Angelina insisted. "You'll be fine."

"Yes, ma'am."

Angelina grinned. "You know a massage would really help you relax."

Miki liked the sound of that. Maybe she had a few extra bucks in her tragically poor bank account to hit one of those fancy spas up near Sara.

"And dirty, filthy monkey sex with a hot guy like Conall is good, too."

Miki slammed her drink down on the table. "All right, let's analyze this, shall we?"

Angelina's head fell back. "Oh, God. Not the analyzin'."

"Let's say I go and have hot monkey sex with the Viking."

Angelina looked at her. "Who?"

"Conall."

"Okay. You do. You work him out of your system and then it's over. And then everybody can go about their day and you can learn to fuckin' relax."

"Problem is that unlike you and Sara, I have a problem with fucking whatever comes along."

"Hey! I think I was insulted. Bitch."

"No, really. I get attached. Emotionally. It's this flaw I have. So, then I'll have to see this fucker every holiday I go up there. He and his wolf buddies will nudge each other and give me that 'I had her' look, while I'm forced to pretend that I'm okay."

"You *have* analyzed this."

"That's what I do, Angelina."

"Fine. You wanna live life alone and bitter, be my guest."

"Trust me. Fucking the Viking isn't going to change the living alone and bitter thing one bit."

"Whatever."

Miki heard them announce final boarding for her flight and the relief nearly floored her. Hopefully by the time Angelina arrived in Northern California, she'd have found a new topic. Miki really would hate to have to kill such a close friend.

"Come on, sassy girl. Let's get your ass on a plane." Angelina finished off her drink.

Miki slipped her computer into her bag and stood up.

Angelina did the same and slammed into a businessman trying to step around their table.

"Sorry, darlin'." Miki *felt* that voice. She looked up and continued to look up at what her grandmother would have termed "a tall drink of water". Once her head was firmly all the way back, she finally saw his face. He was breathtakingly handsome. Dark, dark hair with hints of red and a few streaks of white, he was definitely their age, maybe a year or two older. Gold eyes with green flecks, the lids slightly slanted. And a sexy smile. Basically, trouble with a penis. But he was well groomed. Clearly wealthy if his ten-thousand-dollar titanium watch and alligator-skin briefcase were any indication. And, not surprisingly, he was interested in Angelina. What was surprising was the two men with him. They looked exactly like him. All brothers apparently. Which meant that somewhere out there a couple existed who created these three gorgeous specimens. Amazing.

"You all right, sugar?" Didn't help that sexy voice was Southern. Miki would place him around the Carolinas or Alabama. Georgia maybe. Wherever he hailed from, guys with Southern accents did things to her and her two friends that any other accent simply couldn't touch.

Angelina stared. "Uh..."

Miki's eyes widened. Never, *ever*, in the twenty years she'd known her, had Angelina been at a loss for words over a man. Any man.

Miki slung the bag over her shoulder. "Sorry about that. We need to get to my plane."

"No problem. Y'all can slam in to me any time."

He may have said "y'all" but he clearly meant only Angelina. Who still hadn't quite found her voice yet. They called Miki's plane again. She had to go or she'd miss her flight and never hear the end of it from Sara.

She couldn't leave Angelina, though. Not with this one. Definitely not with all three.

"Hey, Ang. We need to go." She grabbed her friend's arm and tugged. When that didn't seem to work, she yanked.

Angelina snapped out of her stupor. "Uh...oh, yeah. Yeah. We better get moving." She glanced at Southern Charm. "Sorry."

"Not at all." Then he and his tailor-made suit walked off. Miki knew it was tailor-made because they simply didn't make suits in that size for off-the-rack. His two brothers, with a leer at Miki, followed.

"You all right?"

"Yeah." Angelina shook her head. "Yeah. I'm fine, dude."

"I couldn't leave you with him, ya know."

"You think every tall guy is either Pride or Pack."

"I don't know what he is. But Sara and her Pack have pissed off some major players."

"And yet you're trotting off to Seattle by yourself."

"First off, I don't trot. Second, I can take care of myself. Always have. Always will. I don't need babysitters. Besides I'm not the one in danger of becoming the love slave of some shapeshifter."

Angelina finally snapped back completely. "You're kidding, right? With Lassie on your tail?"

"Shut up."

ॐ

Conall checked his watch. Again. Soon his personal wet fantasy would be here. He wondered if it would be inappropriate to tackle her in the hallway as soon as she arrived and drag her up to his bedroom. Probably. Damn human etiquette.

He heard the glass doors leading to the back of the house slide open, and then he heard Zach. "Either you control that mutt or I'll have him go play fetch on the freeway. Your choice, woman." He slammed the door shut.

Zach walked over to Conall and, with a heavy sigh, sat

down on the bench beside him.

Conall wasn't buying it for a second. "Don't even try and pretend like she annoys you."

"She's making my life a living hell."

"She's the best thing to ever happen to this Pack. And God knows, she's the best thing to ever happen to *you*."

"Yeah, I know." Sara Morrighan had only been Zach's mate and the Pack's Alpha Female for six months, but it had been the best six months the Pack had known for years. She wasn't normal. Even by wolf standards. But her odd view of everything was infectious. The females worshipped her and feared her in equal amounts while the males knew not to push her patience. Still, they appreciated that she took the jagged edges off Zach. He was still a ball buster, but a much friendlier one. She'd even gotten the respect of the older wolves who didn't live in the main house, which was usually damn near impossible.

Conall checked his watch and Zach chuckled.

"How long before she gets here?"

"Two hours. Six minutes. And thirty-four seconds."

"Well, I'm glad you're not all wound up about it."

Oh, I'm wound all right. Tight. He never stopped thinking about her. Wanting her. He was dying to know exactly what kinds of things got her off. Sucking her nipples? Licking her clit? Or something more simple? His hands in her hair? His tongue in her ear?

Zach had thrown every available female from the club scene at him. He wanted Conall to lose interest in what he termed "Sara's big-mouthed friend," but none of the women held his interest. Conall only wanted Miki. And he couldn't wait until he had her tight little butt naked and on his lap.

"She'll come around," he stated with as much conviction as

possible.

"She's human, Conall. You should go for a nice wolf girl."

Conall looked over at his best friend and the Alpha Male of the Magnus Pack. Bite marks and bruises riddled the man's body. And Conall knew from when they shifted after hunting that claw marks covered the man's back. It was true, Sara rocked Zach's world. But she also chewed the shit out of him while doing it. Conall would rather have sex that didn't involve bloodletting. At least not as much. "I'm not looking for marriage here, Zach. I just want to fuck her until one of us dies."

"Well...that's a goal. But if you ask me she's rude. Loud. Short."

"She's direct. Confident. Petite."

"Man, do you have it bad."

Conall didn't bother denying it because they both knew it was true.

"By the way." He decided to change the subject since talking about Miki only made him hard. "We had some visitors on our property last night."

He could feel Zach tense next to him. His only objective was to protect his mate. Zach would destroy anyone who threatened her.

"Who?"

"Not sure. But it's the same scent as the one from the rave."

"Great. Just what I fucking need."

"They weren't here long. Jake's stupid but he was on them pretty fast."

"On who pretty fast?"

Conall and Zach looked up to see Sara standing in front of them, a stack of mail in her hand. She'd really gotten stealthy lately, learning how to stay downwind.

"Nothing," Zach grunted.

Sara sighed and squeezed in between the two of them on the bench. "You're lying to me. I really hate that." She laid her head on Zach's shoulder. "You might as well tell me now, mate. I'll just get it out of you later."

"I'm never sure if those are threats or promises."

With a low growl, she bit Zach's shoulder. Zach winced as she drew blood. "It's both." She retracted her canines.

Conall knew if he didn't say anything he'd have to witness the Alpha pair's idea of foreplay—wrestling. All they were missing were the ring and the announcer.

"Something in our territory last night. Not sure what, though."

"Bunnies?" she asked hopefully, and Conall heard Zach growl.

He laughed. Sara always made him laugh. She was a wacky girl.

"Probably not. Not too many bunny shifters."

"So you say. Well, whatever was in our territory should be dead. Are they dead, Conall?"

Zach and Conall looked at Sara, then at each other. The woman was dangerous. She didn't tolerate outsiders on the Pack's property. She didn't tolerate threats to her Pack. She didn't tolerate anything she deemed a danger to who and what she loved. She wasn't a hunter like Conall or Kelly or any of the other Pack members. Sara Morrighan was a stone-cold killer. She knew it and she liked it.

"No, but Jake scared them off."

"I want Angie and Miki safe when they're here."

"They will be," Zach assured her.

"And you better stay close to Miki for me, Conall. You know, for safety."

Zach groaned. "Very subtle, mate."

"I don't know what you mean. I'm only thinking about my friend's safety." If you didn't know her, you would have thought she was being completely sincere.

Sara handed a stack of mail to Zach. "Here." Then she handed a small, card-sized envelope to Conall.

Zach examined the stack in his hand. "Why are there bite marks on these?"

"Roscoe got to the postman before I could."

There was that deep sigh Zach seemed to do a lot since Sara came into his life. He also rubbed his eyes with his palms, making Sara smile and wink at Conall.

"Did he bite the postman?"

"No. He just ripped the mail from his hand. And then the postman ran away—like a little girl."

"Get rid of that dog."

"No."

Conall opened his envelope while Zach and Sara had their weekly fight over "the dog" as Zach called him. He glanced at the card, crumpled it up, and tossed it into the bushes. It took him a minute to realize he now had Zach and Sara's full attention.

"Everything okay?"

Conall shrugged at Zach's question. "It's from my cousin."

Just like that, Zach stopped caring. He knew Conall's family, and he didn't like them. So, he began to open the stack of bills. Sara, however, was a different story. You couldn't put off her curiosity with a crowbar.

"What's wrong with your cousin?"

"Nothing."

"Again with the lying. You know I hate that."

Zach grinned at that.

"What was the card about?"

"He wants me to visit the family. But I think I'd rather set myself on fire."

"That seems extreme. And unnecessary. We're your family. Fuck them." Sara Morrighan was quite the delicate flower. "Do you want to go see them?"

"No."

"Then I'm forbidding you to go. Because I'm Alpha Female and, apparently, I can do that." Not that she ever would unless he wanted her to. Right now, though, he wanted her to.

"Damn you, woman," he playfully chastised. "I guess I'm stuck here, huh, Zach?"

"I'm not facing those friends of hers on my own."

"What did I say?" Sara snapped. "I want you to be cheery when you see my friends."

"I don't do cheery."

"You will if you want to *do* me."

To Zach's annoyance, Conall laughed at that. The woman never gave Zach an inch. And Conall knew Zach wouldn't have it any other way.

Sara turned back to Conall. "Now I'm insisting you be here because my birthday's coming up and I expect a party. I'm thinkin' Texas barbeque and line dancing."

Zach growled again. "I am *not* line dancing."

Conall nodded. "Then line dancing it is!" He ignored Zach's glare as Sara bumped Conall with her shoulder and he bumped her back. The woman was like the psychotically dangerous little sister he never had.

Staring at the paperwork in his hand, Zach snarled, "What the fuck is going on with this friggin' water bill?"

∞

Miki stepped out of the limo and stared. "Are you sure this is the right address?"

"Yes, ma'am. I do all the pickups for Mr. Sheridan."

"But this isn't a house." A mansion. A castle. A palace. But not a house.

"I'll get your bags, ma'am."

Miki nodded as she continued to stare at Sara's new home. A huge building on its own sprawling range of land. Next to the house was an enormous garage filled to overflowing with choppers of every shape and description as well as a couple of pickup trucks and SUVs. She recognized Marrec's bikes immediately. Seemed the Pack was giving Sara's surrogate dad a ton of business.

She couldn't believe this. How could Sara be living here? Sara who was happy with a book and soda. Sara who happily worked at Marrec's place for fifteen years and "C'd" her way right through high school and junior college. How could that Sara now be living in a place where the drive from the gate to the house alone took almost ten minutes?

Miki remembered one of Angelina's last comments to her: "You'll like her place. It's nice. Just needs a porch."

A porch?

The front door opened and Sara appeared. Physically, she was a little different. Leaner. Her hair much longer, almost to her waist. But she was still Sara with her worn jeans, battered Harley-Davidson T-shirt, and old cowboy boots. Sara's face lit up as soon as she saw Miki and Miki hated herself for waiting so long to come see her friend.

"Dude!" Sara charged down the stairs and straight to the limo, tackling Miki and knocking them both back into the vehicle.

Sara's laughter and excitement were infectious and, before Miki knew it, she was hugging her friend back and squealing right along with her.

"You bitch! I thought you'd never come!" Sara stood, grabbed Miki's hand, and dragged her back out of the car. She hugged her again.

At the same time they both said, "Your hair's longer."

Then they started laughing.

"Where would you like me to put the bags, Mrs. Sheridan?"

Sara froze, a vicious growl bubbling up from low in her gut. "The name is Ms. Morrighan. You call me Mrs. again and I will squeeze your balls until you're dead. Now throw the fuckin' bags in the hall."

"Yes, ma'am." The driver hustled Miki's bags away.

"Well, I'm glad to see you finally got your aggression under control."

Arms around each other they walked back toward the house. "I think he does that shit on purpose."

"What's the big deal? You are going to marry him, right?"

"Why?" And Sara actually meant that. "I mean, we're marked. It's not like either of us is going anywhere. Besides..." She held up her right arm, a stunning tribal tattoo covered most of it. "We got matching ink."

Sara and Zach were definitely an interesting couple. Miki

was still recovering from Sara's call five months before when she excitedly told her friend she and Zach had "done the deed". Miki thought that meant they'd rushed off to get married. But leave it to Sara...they'd both gone to the hospital and gotten sterilized. Perfectly matched shapeshifters who never wanted to breed. It was kind of sweet in a bizarre paranormal kind of way.

"Such a beautiful declaration of love. You're like rock stars now."

"Sarcastic bitch. God, I missed that."

Sara grabbed Miki's jacket and dragged her into the house. Miki had never seen Sara with so much energy. And the woman couldn't stop smiling. Finally Sara found where she belonged and Miki couldn't be happier for her.

"So whatcha think of the house?"

"I think it's a fuckin' mansion."

"Yeah, I guess. But it needs a porch."

Once inside, Miki gawked, her mouth open in awe. It was more amazing inside than out. Their hallway actually had marble floors and mile-high ceilings. A winding stairway sat opposite from the huge oak doors that led into the sunken living room.

"Your room is up those stairs. Second door on the left. This is the living room. It's got a gigantic TV. I watch all the football games on that." Sara dragged her down the hallway. "This here's the kitchen. Nice, huh?"

"Shame you can't cook."

"Excuse me, but I make a mean chicken and dumplings."

"And that's all you make."

Miki suddenly found herself in another Sara hug. The girl had really gotten strong and clearly hadn't quite learned how to control it. Much more and she'd crack Miki's ribs.

"I missed you so much."

"Sara—"

"And I can't wait until Angie gets here. Then the three of us will be back together again."

"You're killing me."

"Oh. Sorry." Sara quickly released her. "Hey. I gotta introduce you to somebody. Hold on." Sara ran outside and Miki looked around the stainless steel kitchen with its Italian tile. She whistled in appreciation.

"I'm glad you like it."

She screamed and jumped back about three feet. "Fuck, Zach! Make some goddamn noise, why don't ya?"

"Get used to it, sweetness. We all do it."

They both sneered at each other.

Zach looked her up and down. "Nice boots."

Miki picked up an orange from a bowl on the counter. She tossed it across the enormous room. "Go get it, boy! Go get it!"

Zach gritted his teeth, his eyes narrowing dangerously. She wondered what Sara had made him promise to keep him from coming across the counter for her. This could prove to be fun.

"So, Zach." She grinned. "Where are your old Alphas, Yates and Casey? Or did you just kill 'em, eat their carcasses, suck the marrow from their bones, and then roll around in your own filth in an orgy of blood and death?"

Zach glared at her.

"What?" She shrugged innocently. "I'm just askin'."

"They're in DC opening a new club, you psychotic little..."

Miki chuckled, ignoring whatever he was calling her and turned back to the glass sliding doors. She saw Sara calling something over.

"Oh, dear God!" Miki spun away, turning to Zach in horror. "What the hell is that?"

"That's her dog."

"Dear God, man, what were you thinking? You can't let that thing in your house. It's a mutant!"

"She found it on the side of the highway. Had to have it."

"What's wrong with it?"

"Nothing, really. Except for his short stubby front legs, his very long back legs, and freakishly large head. His sloping back. And, of course, he's missing an eye."

Sara returned, tragically with the dog. "And this is your Aunt Miki." Miki stared down at the beast. "Mik. This is Roscoe T. Budsworth."

"Roscoe T. Budsworth? That's the best you could do?"

"That's a wonderful name. It has prestige."

Zach looked down at the dog. "No matter what you call him that is still one ugly fucking dog."

Sara glared at Zach as she leaned over and covered up Roscoe's long, floppy ears. "You be nice to him!"

"You're lucky I'm being nice to her." Zach glared at Miki. "Later, Tinker Bell."

"Later, jackoff."

With one last glare, Zach walked out of the kitchen.

Sara crouched down next to Roscoe and rubbed his shiny coat. "You told him to go fetch, didn't you?"

"I didn't actually use those words..."

Chapter Three

Miki fell face first onto her bed. Huge and so soft, it would be like sleeping on clouds. And it smelled wonderful. She buried her nose into the comforter and breathed in deep. Okay. She'd admit it. A body could get used to living like this. Easily.

She'd spent the last four hours with Sara in the kitchen. They ate biscuits and drank buttermilk while playing with that amazingly sweet, but disturbing-to-look-at dog.

And not once had Conall stopped by. Which was good, dammit. No matter what Sara and Angelina thought, she wasn't about to hook up with Conall Víga-Feilan, present-day Viking. No way. No day.

She'd learned the hard way that love and sex and all the rest of it was bullshit. A distraction from the bigger picture. Her mother had been planning on college in the hopes of going to medical school. Then she'd met Miki's father. One illegitimate baby later and she was working herself to death to put food on the table while her own mother took care of Miki. But Miki had no intention of going down that road. So her bigger picture would be the next three days. Everything else would take a back seat to that.

At the moment, the Pack was downstairs ordering Chinese food and Miki had taken the opportunity to come up to her room and take a shower. She felt grungy after her day in the airport and on the plane, and she still had a full night planned. They were all going to one of the Pack's clubs for some serious dancing and partying. She'd tried to back out of it, but Sara fought her hard, insisting that Miki needed to relax.

But Miki couldn't relax until she was done. And since she would probably only get two or three hours of sleep anyway, killing some time at a club couldn't hurt.

She thought about the Pack. They were all so sweet to her...except Zach. And they seemed to really love Sara...especially Zach. She got the feeling life with the old Alphas, Yates and Casey, was a little too stifling for the Pack. Zach tossed around the phrase "free choice" a lot, and Sara didn't like to be bothered with what everybody was up to as long as the Pack remained protected.

Miki realized now she'd foolishly stayed away from her friend all these months. Being back with Sara, talking and bullshitting, was all she really needed to make her feel one hundred percent better. Now she felt ready to defend her dissertation and start her new life.

That, however was a concern for later. Right now Miki wasn't ready to do too much of anything. So, still lying face down, she tried to kick off her shoes. Unfortunately, they were boots and she'd laced them up pretty tight. She grumbled in annoyance and for some idiotic reason kept trying to kick one off with the help of the other, feeling way too lazy to actually get up and take her shoes off like a civilized person.

But when she felt strong, firm hands wrap around her boot and begin to unlace it, she jerked in surprise. Pushing herself up on her hands, Miki looked over her shoulder. Conall was at the foot of the bed—on his knees—untying her laces. She had no idea how long he'd been standing there watching her, but her entire body got warm at the thought.

"Hey, Miki." He didn't look up, simply kept untying her laces. And, even though he couldn't see the fronts of her boots, was probably taking a lot longer than actually necessary.

"Hey, Conall."

"How's it going? You have a good trip?"

Miki had to swallow to get the words out. "Yeah." Okay. One word. Apparently she couldn't manage any better at the moment. All the guy was doing was helping her off with her boots. Of course, he was on his knees doing it. She kind of liked him on his knees.

Get a grip, Kendrick.

She needed to start talking. Now. "How's it going with you?"

He still didn't look up; instead, watching his own big hands slowly remove one boot then start on the other. His hair, thick and almost white blond, fell in front of his face. Like hers, it was longer than when she last saw him, just brushing across his shoulders. His hair reminded her of silk and she wondered if it would feel that way against her skin.

"Pretty good," he murmured softly.

He slid the other boot off and placed it aside. Leaning back on his haunches, he ran his hands over her calves and feet while staring at her face. He had the lightest blue eyes she'd ever seen and they completely mesmerized her.

"Anything else you need help taking off?" he asked gruffly.

Miki almost said "everything" but caught herself. She pulled her feet away from Conall's wonderful touch and pulled herself up to her knees. Smirking, she gave a little wave. "No. I'm fine. But thanks." He slowly stood, his eyes never leaving her face. Still on her knees, she moved back away from him as his body kept rising. She'd forgotten exactly how tall he was. And exactly how big. In some respects, the man *was* a bear.

So busy staring and trying to stay away from him, Miki fell right off the bed.

"Miki?" She looked up to find him on the bed, hovering over her. "Are you okay?" He didn't even try to stifle his laughter. Great. Now he could see exactly the level of her geekiness. It was off the charts, she knew. Well, that should convince him she was definitely not the woman for him. A guy like Conall should get some vacuous supermodel babe who couldn't complete a full sentence or even spell sentence.

"I'm fine." She sat up, but before she could struggle to her feet, Conall moved around the bed to stand behind her. His big hands slid under her arms and lifted her off the floor as if she weighed no more than a bag of chips.

"Uh...thanks," she bit out as her feet touched solid ground. She tried to pull away from him, but he wasn't letting her go. Instead, he pulled her back until he held her against his chest. His arms slid around her body and he leaned in close, gently trapping her arms against her sides. If this were anybody else, she would have completely flipped out. They'd be lucky if they had their eyes when she was done. But she couldn't even concentrate when Conall had his hands on her.

Husky, against her ear. "I missed you, Mik."

The man was killing her. "Conall?"

"Miki?" He nuzzled her neck as one of his—*huge!*—hands slid over her breast. Immediately, her nipples hardened. She blinked. *When the hell did that start happening?*

"I think you need to back off." At least she was pretty sure she said that. She was having trouble concentrating. Especially with his tongue sliding up across her neck to her ear.

"You *think*?" His hand squeezed her breast and her back arched. "Or you *know*?"

Oh boy, he's good. Miki bet that with very little effort,

Conall could turn a nun into a whore. Of course, she wasn't a nun.

She yanked her body away from his and it was as if her skin started to yell at the loss of him.

Miki backed away. "Conall. Don't get the wrong idea."

"And what idea is that?"

"I'm not going to sleep with you."

He took a step toward her. "I am so not talking about sleeping."

She backed up again. "You're not going to make this easy on me, are you, Viking?"

He took another step forward. "Not on your life, Kendrick."

She backed up once again and slammed into a dresser. She held her arm up as if to ward him off. "Stay!"

And he did.

"Look, you're an unnaturally large, good-looking guy. I'm sure there are a plethora of women out there who would be perfect for you."

"Personally, I like women who can successfully use 'plethora' in a sentence."

Dammit, the bastard made her smile. She hated that. Especially when he smiled back. He was truly gorgeous. And as dangerous as they come.

Forcing her smile under control, "I'm going to take a shower. So you need to piss off." She walked to the bathroom and as she stepped into the luxurious and huge room, she realized Conall stood behind her. Okay. Now this was just getting creepy.

She turned around. "Is there something else?"

"No. Not at all."

"Okay. Well, I'm going to take a shower...by myself."

"Great." They stared at each other. She couldn't understand what the fuck he was grinning at. Then, finally, with a low chuckle he asked, "You do know this is my bathroom?"

Miki closed her eyes. "What?"

"Yeah. In fact, this is *my* room."

She gritted her teeth. Great. That wonderful smell on the neatly made bed had been Conall. And who the fuck made their bed these days anyway? Miki didn't make her bed unless she was changing the sheets.

"She told me it was the second door on the right."

"Actually, yours is third. Right next door."

"Of course it is." She would *kill* Sara.

"But, please, feel free to stay. Take all the showers you want. I can help with the soap."

Images of that danced through her besotted brain and it felt as if someone squeezed her lungs because she was having a lot of trouble breathing.

"Well, that's very neighborly of you, Viking. But I'll just go to my own room."

He wasn't completely blocking her way, but she had to slide against him to get out of the bathroom and she felt that connection all the way down to her toes. She almost moaned.

"Well, see you at dinner," she squeaked out.

Then she ran.

Conall didn't care how his Alpha felt about it; he was going to give Sara the biggest kiss he could. Coming back to his room only to find his ultimate sexual fantasy spread eagle, face down on his bed was more than any man could ask for. Would dare hope for. And when she started smelling his comforter, he thought he might come in his jeans.

The woman did things to him without even trying. It seemed like he had no self-control around her. When he first saw her, he'd had no intention of touching her. In fact, he'd purposely stayed away when she arrived. Sara told him if he met Miki at the airport or greeted her at the door, she'd freak. So he wanted to give her a chance to relax before he pounced. But once he smelled her again, he just couldn't keep his hands off her.

If this got any worse, he might start humping her leg.

He closed his bedroom door and took a deep breath. Just the scent of her got him hard. And it didn't help she looked so good. It had only been six months, but he was positive she actually looked even hotter. Her curly hair a little longer, now reaching just above her shoulders, and her skin looked as soft if not softer than when he last saw her.

Miki simply looked...beautiful. And her body felt amazing. When he held her and when she brushed up against him on her way out the door—he kept imagining that body naked and in all sorts of positions with his.

And the thought of her in his shower. With him soaping those breasts, those legs, that ass.

Damn. Wrong thought, he growled to himself as he headed to his shower.

ॐ

Miki had just pulled on a pair of sweatpants and a sweatshirt, pushing her wet hair out of her face, when Sara knocked on her door and stuck her head in.

"Hey. Dinner's here."

Miki grabbed Sara by her T-shirt, snatched her into the room, and slammed the door.

"What the hell?"

"You sent me to Conall's room, you bitch!"

"Did I? Huh. How did I make that mistake?" Sara ducked as a bottle of shampoo flew at her head. "Jesus Christ, woman! Calm yourself!"

"Stop trying to set me up with him!"

"I'm just trying to get you laid... Put it down!" Miki debated whether to chuck the hairbrush in her hand at her best friend. After a good thirty seconds, she lowered her arm and Sara smiled. "So you went to his room. What's the big deal?"

Miki glared. "He found me face down on his bed smelling his comforter."

Sara choked then exploded into laughter. Miki raised her brush again. "Okay. Okay. I'm sorry. Dude, I'm so sorry. I didn't think you'd get so...comfortable so quickly."

"Bottom line is you and Angelina need to back off."

Sara took a deep breath. "Darlin', I don't see the problem. He's hot. He's straight. He's disease free. Next to my Zach he's walking perfection. What is the deal?"

"The deal is guys like him suck you in, make you theirs, then fuck you over. It's like in their DNA or something."

"Now you're talking about your father."

"I prefer the term sperm donor. And I'm not going to end up like my mother."

"Of course not. Especially 'cause you're not a sixteen-year-old virgin, screwed over by a rich townie, and left pregnant. So, already you're ahead of the game."

Miki glared at Sara's sarcasm. "I already had this goddamn conversation with Angelina. And if you two whores want to have meaningless sex with some guy you just met—like getting head at a rave from a biker—that's your choice."

"Hey! That's not fair. And it was hardly meaningless. I'm practically married to the guy."

"Don't care. Back off."

Sara sighed. "Fine. Fine. I'll back off."

"Thank you."

And Sara backed off for a total of fifteen seconds. "Although a vibrator does not a life partner make."

Miki growled. "Why are you two obsessed with Mr. Happy?"

"Maybe because you actually named it."

"Whatever." Miki turned back to her suitcase, stopping when she saw something she knew she didn't pack. She pulled out a brown paper bag. "Dude, I didn't pack this." Visions of international spies using her as a transporter flew through her mind. But the expression on Sara's scarred face told a different story.

"*You* may not have packed it..."

Miki frowned and opened the bag. There were boxes of condoms inside. And a note lay right on top. Immediately, she recognized Angie's perfect handwriting.

Really, isn't it time you got laid? —Angie.

"I hate both of you."

"Now. Now." Sara backed up toward the door. "Angie and I only want you to be safe. You're not on any birth control.

Sometimes people get lost in the moment. Angie did it with the best of intentions. We care about you and want you to be happy."

"Fuck her. Fuck you. And, for that matter, fuck your intentions."

"See. Those are the tense cuss words of a woman who needs to get laid."

Sara ducked the bag of condoms just in time, tore the door open and ran.

Miki sat on the edge of her bed and dropped her head in her hands. This was going to be a long, long trip.

Chapter Four

"Forget it."

Sara shrugged. "Okay. You can ride with Zach."

"In hell."

Sara didn't answer Zach's bark. She just reached back and punched him in the chest.

"I'm not riding with..." Miki smiled sweetly, "...*him*."

"Then you better get your ass over there."

Miki glanced over at Conall. He leaned against his bike, looking as casual and innocent as always. It didn't help he wore black jeans, black boots, black tee, and a black leather jacket. He looked fucking phenomenal in all black.

He gave her that innocent smile and she couldn't stop the little whimper that came out. She knew without a doubt Conall would not make this easy.

"Would you just go?" Sara spun Miki around and shoved her toward Conall. Immediately, Miki saw the predatory gleam in his eye, but she wouldn't let him see her being weak. Not if she could help it anyway. So, steeling her resolve, she marched over to him.

"All right, Viking, a few ground rules."

He seemed curious. "Such as?"

"No inappropriate touching. No grinding yourself into me. No leaning back into me. No doing stunts on your bike so that I have to grip you tighter. Are we clear?"

Conall chuckled. "I keep forgetting you were raised around bikers." He leaned in to her. She recognized his scent from the comforter. She really liked that scent. *Damn him.* "Look, sweetness, just get your tight ass on the bike."

Miki glared at him. "Maybe I don't want to go."

His head was so close to her it almost touched her cheek. Almost. "We can stay here if you want. I'm sure we can come up with all sorts of things to do in this big house. Alone." Then he leaned in closer and sniffed her. She felt a bolt of electricity going right from her groin up her spine and landing somewhere in the back of her neck. "God, woman," he groaned. "You smell good."

She stumbled back away from him but he caught her arm.

With a firm grasp on her, he straddled his bike and gently pulled her close. "Get on."

She forced herself to slide on the seat behind him and took the helmet he handed to her.

Bastard. He was getting to her and he knew it. She put the helmet on her head, tightened the strap. He kick-started his bike and waited. She knew he was waiting for her, but she didn't know why.

"What?" she demanded over the roar of the chopper's engine.

"You going to put your arms around me or what?"

"I was thinking 'or what'."

He leaned back against her and immediately her nipples hardened. Already he was breaking one of her rules. "Either you put your arms around me or I start poppin' wheelies on this thing." And she knew he meant it.

With a silent groan, she wrapped her arms around his waist. He pulled her tighter, making sure her chest was right against his back, which didn't help the hard nipple situation one damn bit.

He pulled out of the driveway and followed the rest of the Pack that had left a minute before.

Who knew this would be so much more difficult than she ever thought it would be? Like a dog with his bone, Conall held on even though she kept saying, "Drop it. Drop it now."

She needed to get to Seattle. And she needed to get away from the Viking before she did something she would regret the rest of her life.

His bike pulled up beside Zach's as they cruised down the street. Miki watched Sara, her friend finally in her element. Arms wrapped around Zach, she yelled something to him over the roar of the motor that made him smile... Well, it was actually more of a leer. The two seemed to truly enjoy each other's company.

Miki sighed with the sudden realization that she envied her best friend.

"You okay back there?"

Again with the wolf hearing. How did any of them feel comfortable doing anything in that house when they could hear everything?

"Mik?"

"I'm fine. I'm fine."

"Liar." He kept one hand on the handlebars while he used the other to rub her arm. "What's up?"

"Just got a lot on my mind."

"You need to learn how to relax. You know, I'm pretty sure I can help with that."

She just bet he could. "No thank you."

"Really? You sure?"

Miki crossed her eyes, but couldn't help but smile. The man really was shameless. "*You* really don't need to do anything for me. Ever."

"Spoilsport."

Chapter Five

Miki didn't know a shapeshifter could be so boring. The man just rambled on and on. About himself. Even his name bored her. Bob. She silently began to call him Bob the King of Boring. She let him ramble as she looked around the club.

True, it wasn't much. But that was because wolves didn't need much. A dark, moody room with a big bar, room to dance, and some alcoves where they could make out with the fellow shapeshifter of their choice. This was neutral ground. A place they could all get together, dance, and have a great time without getting territorial.

Of course, this wasn't the entire club, merely the wolf part. One flight down was one of the hottest clubs in Northern California. A place where the rich and famous met up with the vapid and thin. She'd read about Sara's club in one of the magazines at the bookstore. The place wasn't only hot, it made money hand over fist, starting new trends. All that shit.

And Miki had finally come to the realization she still had a hard time dealing with.

Sara was fucking rich. Not a little rich. Not sort of rich. *Fucking* rich.

According to Kelly, her new little Pack confidant, Sara not only had Pack money access, she had money left to her by her parents. Her grandmother refused to touch it, forcing her granddaughter instead to work for every little thing she ever got. Although, Miki was kind of glad about that. She could imagine a rich, snotty shapeshifter Sara. Miki probably wouldn't be friends with that Sara. But cool, still wearing her Jockey For Her underwear Sara was definitely her friend. Her best friend. Just like Angelina.

It was apparently this Sara who had become quite the truce maker, too, pulling together Packs that at one time couldn't stand each other.

Miki's eyes searched the dance floor until she found her. She still couldn't believe six months ago this was the girl who could barely walk, was in constant pain, and lonely beyond belief. As much as Miki envied her now, she felt overwhelming happiness for her, too. Miki watched as Sara, her favorite black cowboy hat in place, moved her body against Zach's. She had grace and precision and, not surprisingly, Zach couldn't keep his hands off her.

It suddenly occurred to Miki that Bob was still rambling. The tragedy with her brain was that she could still listen to him even when she was thinking about twenty different other things. Her grade school teachers called it a gift. Gift her ass, if she had to listen to Bob talk about how great he was all night. Thank God he wasn't part of Sara's Pack.

Of course, that fact didn't seem to stop Bob from moving in on her. He'd gotten closer and she didn't like it one bit. She felt naked with only her steel-toe Docs. Because she had to take a plane into Northern California, she had to leave all her precious weapons back home. Miki had learned a long time ago a woman her size definitely needed an advantage.

She glanced around for a beer bottle to smash and then use on Bob should it become necessary, but then Conall suddenly stalked out of the crowd. He grabbed Bob by the back of the neck and slammed his head down on the bar, then lifted him up and tossed him, sending the man flying across the floor and hitting the opposite wall.

Conall grinned as he sat his big body down on the stool next to her. The one he'd just forced poor Bob to leave. "So, you having a good time?"

Apparently, they wouldn't be discussing Conall's way of getting a man to back off. She wondered briefly if he'd done that because Bob was making her uncomfortable or because Bob was making him uncomfortable being so close to her. She hated herself for hoping it was both.

"Yeah. Downstairs sucks, but this place is great."

"This is for family only." And she knew he saw all wolves as his family. For some unknown reason she liked that.

"You want something to drink?"

"Water." Miki watched as he leaned over and spoke to the bartender. Man, was his body long. Long and big. He'd taken off his jacket and stowed it along with hers behind the bar. He wasn't dark like Zach. But at the same time he wasn't pale. He wore a black sleeveless T-shirt and she marveled at the size of his shoulders and arms. She focused on the thin black bracelet he wore on his wrist. It looked like something a kid made. A couple of pieces of wool braided together. Yet, it had to be the sexiest thing she'd ever seen *in her life*. She couldn't explain it. It just was.

Okay. She needed to stop this right now. *Right now.*

Miki slid off the stool she'd been perched on and stretched her neck. Her whole body felt tight. Tight and cranky. Angie was right. Miki was a tense mess. But she had so much on her mind. She hadn't been bullshitting when she told Conall that. She had more on her mind than anyone could possibly imagine.

A bottle of water suddenly appeared in front of her face and she realized she'd drifted to stand in front of Conall. The thought of him watching her stretch her neck and shoulders made her warm. Again. She needed to get control of that. She had enough on her mind without worrying about uncontrollable hot flashes.

Miki grabbed the water and looked up to find Conall hovering over her. "Christ, you're tall. Is everyone in your family so fuckin' tall?"

"It's the Nordic thing."

It was funny, the music was amazingly loud, but the wolves had no trouble hearing each other. She, however, couldn't hear shit over the industrial techno blasting from the speakers unless someone screamed at her.

Miki drank some of the water and tried to ignore Conall standing behind her. She could feel the heat coming off his body, and it was starting to feel really nice.

Conall stared at the back of Miki's neck. Watching her stretch the tight muscles there and in her shoulders almost sent him over the edge.

She wore a tight tank top, and he could easily see how long and refined her neck was, her shoulders small but strong, her back straight and lightly muscled. He could tell Miki was a girl who knew how to handle herself. He liked that. Liked the fact that she wasn't a little wimp waiting for some knight to come rescue her. By the time the knight made it up to the tower of the castle, she'd have devised an elaborate pulley system to extract herself to safety. He found her brain so sexy. Well, her brain and that ass.

Unable to resist, he took his thumb and stroked the back of her neck. She stiffened but she didn't knock his hand away. Taking that as a good sign, he continued to knead the tense muscles of her neck and watch her body's response. It didn't take her long to relax a little, so he let the rest of his hand settle against her throat. His fingers spread out across her collarbone, gently stroking the sensitive flesh there.

Her back was still to him, but he was almost positive she'd closed her eyes when she dropped her head forward. He massaged other areas of her neck where he felt tightness, keeping it up until he heard her moan. And that sound almost killed him.

Gently, Conall pulled her body into his, her back against his front. Wearing her low-heeled Doc Martens, the top of her head just about reached his chest. Yeah, he could make that height work quite nicely for them both.

He leaned down next to her ear. "Wanna dance?"

She turned and stared at him. "Are you kidding?"

He wondered if she was concerned with the fact she was an amazingly lousy dancer. "What's the problem?"

"I'm not even five-five and what are you? Nine feet or so? We'll look like idiots."

"I am *not* nine feet." He moved around in front of her, finally releasing the hold he had on her neck. For a split second, she actually appeared disappointed.

"You know, Kendrick, I'm unimpressed."

"With what exactly?"

"I thought you brilliant types were a lot more creative." She frowned but that quickly changed into a look of surprise as he bent down, slid his hands under her ass, and lifted her off the floor. She wore a sexy leather miniskirt and he could feel the panties underneath. *Satin. Nice.*

"Are you nuts? Put me down!" But she was smiling and didn't seem all that pissed.

"No way. We're going to dance. Wrap your arms around my neck." She did that quickly since he pretended to almost drop her. "Good girl. And wrap your legs around my waist."

She raised an eyebrow and smirked.

"Get your mind out of the gutter, Kendrick." She rolled her eyes, but wrapped her legs around him just the same. Her ankles locked at the small of his back and her pelvis pushed against his groin. And he wished with all his heart they were back in his room doing this. Naked.

Miki couldn't believe she hadn't punched him yet. She should have. But, she grudgingly had to admit, he felt really good between her legs.

Staring straight at her, he walked them both to the middle of the dance floor. It was awkward for Miki, his heated gaze tearing right through her. No one had ever looked at her like that before. At least not so she'd noticed. She didn't know what to say or do in such a situation, so she glanced around the room instead. She felt him move and her eyes almost rolled into the back of her head. She *liked* how he moved. She briefly wondered if he moved like that in bed.

Bad thought. Bad thought. Bad thought.

She caught sight of Sara watching her. She expected her to be all cocky and triumphant but, instead, she gave Miki the sweetest look, which only made it worse. She didn't want to get Sara's hopes up over nothing.

She knew Sara cared. The woman had cared about her since she'd picked Miki up off the playground floor all those years ago after some evil little boys had knocked Miki down and called her a freak. Sara'd helped her up and Angelina had kicked their asses. She smiled at the memory of those boys running for their lives by the time sweet, girly Angelina had gotten done with them. Since then they'd been protecting each other. Even risking their lives for each other. But sometimes Sara and Angelina's concern for her could get a little stifling.

The skin of her neck was nipped and she turned her head to look at Conall, that aqua blue gaze of his trapping her immediately. *He is sooo trouble.*

"Where did you just go?"

"What?"

"Come on, Mik. You were two thousand miles away. Where'd ya go?"

"Nowhere." She shook her head for emphasis. "Just thinking."

"You do that a lot, huh?"

"Yeah. I guess."

"Like what? What do you think about?"

"You don't want to know, Viking."

"I like when you call me that."

Well, that was the last thing she wanted to hear. She called him that to annoy him. *You idiot, what guy gets insulted being called Viking?*

"You really want to know what I'm thinking?" Perfect. She knew exactly how to scare him off. It had scared off many men before him.

"I asked, didn't I?"

"I was thinking Sara needs to stop looking so happy about us dancing together. And I wondered if Zach was going to fuck her on the dance floor or whether he'd wait to drag her off to the bathroom. He's had his hand down the back of her jeans and his groin pressed into hers for the last ten minutes. I was also wondering whether I should wear my blue suit to my dissertation defense or my dark green suit. Or if I should wear a suit at all. Or just a dress. Then I remembered that I don't have a dress. Then I was wondering if I were hungry or not. I decided not. Then I wondered if I could come up with a way to cancel the government's deficit without taxing the people."

Conall, not surprisingly, stared. "Wow."

"Well, as you said, you asked, didn't you?"

"As a matter of fact, I did." He studied her closely. "Do you ever *not* think? Or, at the very least, only have one thought at a time?"

Miki thought about that for a moment and shook her head. "No."

"Really?"

"I don't distract easily."

The Viking leered and she had that ancient China feeling again. "I bet I could distract you."

With a snort, and before she could stop herself, "Promises, promises." Miki froze and so did Conall. "Uh..."

"Too late. Can't take it back now."

"But..."

"Nope. The gauntlet has been laid." She felt his hands tighten on her ass and she let out a little squeak. "And I'm just the man to pick it up and run with it."

Okay. Exactly at what point did her nipples start hardening without it being cold or someone actually rubbing them? Plus, much more of this, she'd have to change her underwear before the night was out. *When the hell did that start happening?* And what happened to her resolve not to get involved with anyone, especially giant shapeshifters?

I should have added his ass to the List!

"You're vibrating."

"I am not!"

"Your *phone* is vibrating." He jokingly tsk-tsk'd her. "Again, we're wallowing in the gutter. What is it with you?"

Suddenly her face felt as hot and uncomfortable as the rest of her.

Pulling the phone off her hip, she held it up. "I need to deal with this."

With obvious reluctance, he slowly lowered her to the ground and led her away from the dance floor. "Make your call. I'll be back in five minutes." She watched Conall walk off toward the bathroom. She liked watching him walk off.

What the hell was she doing? This was ridiculous. *She* was ridiculous. She should be worrying about her dissertation not about how his ass looked in those jeans.

Miki flipped her phone open. "Hello?"

She knew from caller ID it was Craig. But the reception sucked in the club. So she closed the phone and headed down the stairs and out of the building.

Chapter Six

Conall washed his hands and thought about Miki naked. That's pretty much all he did these days. Think about one small woman naked. There had never been a woman before Miki who distracted him this much. He and Zach had burned their way through a lot of strippers, waitresses and bar sluts. Girls who knew how to get you hot and suck you off in no time. Girls who really didn't expect you to call them the next morning.

Miki wasn't anything like those girls. She was hot and sexy without even trying. She never wore makeup from what he could tell and she didn't need any. She wore those same damn Doc Martens every time he saw her and he wasn't sure she had any other shoes. But she always seemed to pair them with the hottest little miniskirt or shorts. Tonight she wore leather. The woman looked really good in leather.

She was a walking, talking contradiction and he was starting to worry he was falling for her. Still, a more skittish female he didn't know. No way could she handle him. Not really.

Conall dried his hands and headed toward the bathroom door. Before he could touch the knob, the door opened in and his almost exact replica followed. But his cousin Einarr had hazel eyes and always looked pissed off. The man wasn't pleasant and, after all these years, Conall still hated his guts.

"Hello, cousin."

ॐ

Miki had to walk away from the club and go half a block down to the corner to get decent reception. She speed-dialed Craig back.

"Whatcha want?" she barked into the phone, her eyes scanning the street.

"That's not friendly."

Craig could be such a bonehead. "Craig."

"Okay. Okay. Just kidding. I only wanted to make sure you were going to be here tomorrow night as planned."

"Yeah. Why?"

"Everybody's psyched about seeing you. Right, guys?"

Miki laughed when she heard chanting from the other end. "Mi-ki! Mi-ki! Mi-ki!"

"Okay. Okay. I'll be there. And you're all idiots."

"Meet us at Patty's Pub."

"When?"

"Anytime after ten. We'll be there until closing." Of course they would. Her Seattle friends were the hardest drinkers she knew. "Don't flake out on us, Queen of Despair and Pain, ruler of the dark underworld known as Texas." Miki closed her eyes. Her friends were such geeks. Which meant she was a big ol' geek herself because they often called her their queen.

"I said I'd be there. Don't pressure me."

"All right, my lovely. See you then."

She hung up her phone and hooked it back to the holster on her hip. Then she wrapped her arms around her body. She was freezing. It got cold at night in Northern California. Why couldn't Sara's Pack live in Southern California where she heard it was warm all the time?

Miki headed back up the street toward the club. As she passed an alley she stopped. She had to. They'd called her name.

She stared into the deep recesses of the dark alley and Miki heard it again. A female voice. A couple. Calling her name. She faced the alley, but didn't enter. She wasn't about to. She wasn't stupid. Instead, she'd go back to the club and get Sara and Zach.

But a hand suddenly grabbed her arm. "Don't leave."

She looked up into the face of a woman...or a man...or a she-male. To be honest, she really didn't know. Pretty but androgynous. Yet with a grip on her arm that caused Miki some serious discomfort.

"Let me go."

"Don't leave, sweetness. We were just ready to get the party started now that you're here."

That's when she tried to drag Miki into the alley. Miki remembered taking a self-defense class once and she never forgot the instructor's words. "Never let them take you to a secondary location. *Never.*"

To Miki that alley *was* a secondary location. No fucking way would she go in there. Reaching up she grabbed the woman's hair—*this was a woman, right?*—and yanked so that they both stumbled back slamming into a parked car. The car's alarm went off while Miki yanked the woman's hair again. Then she did it again until she ripped hair from the heifer's head. The woman let out a screech that would have freaked Miki out if she wasn't busy trying not to get taken to the secondary location. Of course, the returning yelps from the alley just spurred her action.

With hair still gripped in her fist, she punched the woman in the face. Then used her steel-toe Docs to kick her in the groin. Man or woman, she knew that would hurt. As the woman dropped to the ground, Miki snatched her arm away and ran.

∞

"What do you want, Einarr?"

"Can't a man just come and see his cousin?"

"No. And you know Zach doesn't want you here." Especially after what happened last time. Wolf blood still stained the walls from that little get-together.

"A lackey for that Irish Wolfhound. How do you look at yourself in the mirror?"

Conall rolled his eyes. They'd been having this conversation for over ten years. It was a boring conversation just as Einarr was a boring man. Truly, the only thing his cousin had inherited from their Viking ancestors was his name and his viciousness. Other than that, he wasn't much of a Viking or a wolf. Just a petty little asshole.

"Move, Einarr."

And to his surprise, Einarr did. Yet Conall never took his eyes off him as he left the bathroom.

Once he made it back to the main bar, he realized they were all over the place. Víga-Feilan wolves. Not good.

Conall walked up to Kelly. "Where's Zach?"

"The office, maybe. I really don't know."

Conall headed off to the office before things spiraled out of control. This was why Zach was Alpha. Left up to Conall, he'd snap his cousin's neck as human and start a Pack-Pack war just before being shipped off to prison. Probably not a good idea. At least for the moment, it wasn't a good idea.

∓

Miki slammed her way back into the club, to the backstairs, and right into the arms of one of the wolves guarding the door.

"Hey. Hey. Are you okay?"

Miki looked behind her. She didn't see anyone following her. She took in huge gulps of air and tried to calm herself down.

"I better get Sara."

Miki grabbed his arm. "Don't you dare!"

She had enough problems. Involve Sara and all hell would break loose. "I'm fine. Really."

"You're bleeding, honey."

Miki glanced down at her forearm. There were four deep gashes across it. *Great. Paw marks.*

"I'll take care of it. I'll be fine." She headed up the stairs, stopping at the bar to get her leather jacket from behind it. She slipped it on and headed to the bathroom. Thankfully, she didn't see Conall or Sara. She could only imagine how the two of them would blow this out of proportion.

She went in search of the women's bathroom, finding it pretty easily. How could she miss it? It was actually marked "Bitches". She went in as some females came out. She went to the sink and caught her reflection in the mirror. Except for being a little sweaty, she still looked in control. Good. She slid the jacket off one arm and ran her forearm under the cold water, wincing from the pain, but thankful the cuts weren't too deep.

She took paper towels and carefully wiped the damaged area. So intent on what she was doing, it took her several minutes to realize that a woman stood behind her—and stared.

Watching her reflection in the mirror, Miki marveled at how much the woman seriously resembled Conall. Funny, he never mentioned a sister. But she kept staring and smirking without saying anything. And Miki was in a considerably foul mood.

"What?" Miki snapped.

"Just trying to figure out what my cousin's doing with a little midget like you."

"Maybe you should ask him that. And calling someone a 'little midget' is redundant. Midget implies little." The woman stared at her and Miki couldn't resist. "I'm sorry, should I speak slower? Perhaps sound words out for you?"

The woman growled as Miki slipped her jacket back on. And, being Miki, she simply couldn't leave it alone. "You know there's no shame in having special needs." She leaned in and whispered conspiratorially, "The short bus can be fun."

With that last shot, she walked out the door, but the woman clamped her hand around her already wounded arm. Miki let out a pained bark, but it only lasted a second. Because suddenly Conall was there, lifting the woman up and slamming her against the far wall.

"I should tear your throat out."

"You don't have the guts, cousin."

Conall growled, his canines extending to deadly points.

Then he heard a snarl and felt hands slide under his arms and loop around the back of his neck. "Let her go or I'll snap your neck."

Einarr. But Conall was too pissed to let his cousin go. She'd hurt Miki. That was all the wolf in him knew. That was all he needed to know.

"Fuck you."

Einarr's grip tightened as Conall distantly heard glass breaking. Then he felt Einarr stiffen.

"Let him go or I cut 'em off."

The three Víga-Feilans looked down. Miki crouched low behind Einarr, a broken bottle shoved between his legs and up against his groin.

"What the fuck?" Einarr wasn't used to women facing off against him. He was big and imposing and used that to his advantage. Clearly, however, Miki didn't care.

"Let him go."

"Get the fuck away from me...hey! Cut that shit out!" Conall would have laughed at his cousin's obvious discomfort if the man hadn't tightened his grip on his throat.

"Miki. Go," Conall ordered.

"No way." She looked around Einarr's legs at Conall. "I'm having way too much fun." She glanced up at Einarr. "You ever seen a horse castrated? I have."

He could smell Einarr's fear and panic. And he loved it. But he wanted Miki safe.

"Hey, Conall. What's going on?" His Alphas. He loved how Sara always seemed so calm. So in control. Seconds before she started to really hurt someone.

"Just a little disagreement."

"Really?" Sara crouched down next to Miki. "Whatcha doin'?"

"Playing let's turn the stallion into a gelding. Of course, in his case I guess it's really turning a dog into a bitch." Conall heard Einarr grunt and knew Miki was having way too much fun with that broken bottle.

"You know, Mik. We can take it from here."

"He's not your Pack, right?"

"Nope."

"Then as a Texan I have no choice but to help out in thanks for your kind hospitality. So until he gets his hands off Conall...his balls are mine."

Sara stood up. "You heard her." She leaned in. "And if I were you, I'd do it. She helped on a ranch for two years when she was twelve. The girl is not afraid to get bloody."

Einarr's hands released Conall.

"Good boy." He could hear the condescension in Miki's voice. "Now sit pretty!"

Sara slapped her hand over Miki's mouth and shoved her back with the rest of the Pack. It amazed him Miki had lived *this* long.

Sara's hand rested on his shoulder. Heard her cool, calm voice in his ear. "Who's this?"

He tried to rein in the beast. If he let it loose now, he'd kill the bitch in front of him. Sara probably smelled that. She knew her Pack well.

"This is my cousin." He released her. "Gudrun Víga-Feilan." That was all he could manage at the moment. Not a problem, though. Sara pushed him back and the two females squared off while he and Einarr continued to glower at each other.

Sara took a protective stance in front of Conall. Kind of funny, since he towered over her. But he'd seen this woman in action. Gudrun, however, had not.

"Pretty scar," his cousin sneered.

He would have launched himself at her again, but Zach

71

grabbed his arm and held him back. He realized Zach didn't want him involved. Not because it was two females fighting, but because the man loved watching Sara do damage. It made him hard.

"Wow. That was witty. I've never heard that one before."

Gudrun's eyes narrowed. Conall could smell his cousin's annoyance that her insults weren't bothering Sara. And they really weren't. The girl had lived with worse for years. Hell, she'd lived with her grandmother for years. That alone made her tough.

So, seeing that Sara wasn't an easy target, Gudrun looked back at him. "That little midget." She glanced in Miki's direction. "So weak. So vulnerable."

Sara snorted. "She almost took your brother's balls off and wore them as ear muffs. And 'little midget' is redundant. Midget implies little, dumb ass."

"I told her that," Miki announced from behind Jake.

Gudrun couldn't stand being made fun of and that weakness seemed to make her irrational or just plain stupid. She punched Sara in the face.

A long stretch of silence followed as Sara stared at Gudrun, her hand rubbing her jaw. Yet leave it to Miki to solidify the moment. "She is going to kick your fat ass."

That's when Sara moved. She grabbed Gudrun and slammed her head first into the wall. Then she brought her back and down while bringing her knee up. He heard his cousin's nose break. Smelled Gudrun's blood. Then Sara wrapped her hand in the woman's short blonde hair and dragged her past them all.

"Time for you to go, sunshine. You and your Pack are no longer welcome." Gudrun's Pack followed closely behind and the Magnus Pack followed the Víga-Feilans. Miki was right next to him as Sara dragged his cousin down the stairs, making sure she hit a few walls and the banister with the woman's head along the way. They went out the side door and spilled into the alley beside the club. That's when Sara lifted the woman up and threw her out on the sidewalk.

She looked at Einarr. "Get this bitch off my territory. I see any of you back here again, I'll kill you. Not them." She motioned to the rest of the Viga-Feilans. "You. Now get the fuck out of my sight." Einarr stared at her. He tried to stare her down, but Sara didn't flinch. She didn't look away. Conall was pretty sure she didn't blink. They could all feel it. That moment when Sara would lose it and tear the man's throat out. No one stared at Sara too long for just that reason. Well, no one but Zach.

Einarr backed away, still staring at Sara. At this point, it was his only way to save face with his Pack.

Carrying Gudrun, the Pack went to their vehicles parked across the street, and disappeared.

Conall closed his eyes. He couldn't look at Sara or Miki. His family never failed to embarrass the living hell out of him.

He felt Sara's cool hand on his cheek. "Hey, stretch. It's okay."

"I'm sorry, Sara."

"I'm the one person you never have to apologize about family to. Remember that."

He smiled at her. How could Zach *not* have fallen in love with her? And, apparently, Zach felt that way, too. He slid his arms around his mate's waist and nuzzled her neck. Then he grabbed her left thigh and just like that tough, fearless Sara freaked.

First she squealed. A real girly squeal. Then she backed away from her mate. "Don't you dare, Zacharias Sheridan!"

"Come here, baby."

She burst out laughing and ran back to the club, Zach following slowly behind her. He didn't have to run. He knew he'd catch her and then he'd drag her back to their office. Probably so he could fuck her brains out.

The Pack looked at each other, then headed back to the club. They'd never understand their Alphas, but in the end they really didn't have to.

Miki looked up at him. "What the hell was that?"

"Do you really want to know?"

Miki went quiet for a second, then shook her head. "Probably not."

"Look, Mik. I'm sorry about my cousins. And thanks for threatening Einarr's balls for me."

Miki shrugged as if she hadn't challenged a man who could have literally ripped her apart. "No problem."

"You know you were protecting me."

"See. There's that Viking grin. And that really unnerves me."

"I don't know what you mean."

"Yes, you do. And what I did in the club doesn't mean anything." He moved toward her and she backed away. He was really starting to enjoy this little dance of theirs.

"It means everything to me."

She took another step back, tripped over her own two feet and fell back. Conall caught her before she hit the ground. Both arms around her, holding her. And that's when he smelled it.

He leaned in and sniffed her again. "Where the hell have you been?"

"Nowhere." She tried to pull away, but he gripped her

tighter. "I smell something...and blood. Are you bleeding?"

"It's that time of the month, is all."

He stared down at her. "Miki. We know the difference between open wounds and menstrual blood. Don't bullshit me."

"Mind your own business, Viking. Now let me go."

She pulled out of his arms and turned to walk away. With a growl, he grabbed her jacket and snatched it off her back. When she spun around to yell at him, he saw the bleeding wounds on her forearm. Something had pawed her. Whatever owned that scent had touched her. Hurt her. And that something wasn't his cousin.

He grabbed Miki around the waist, ignoring her "You asshole! Get your hands off me!" And carried her back into the club.

Chapter Seven

Conall held her close to his side. He could smell her blood. He could smell *them*. They'd touched her. They'd touched what he considered his.

He took her back to the Pack part of the club. As soon as they walked in, all the wolves stopped and looked at him and Miki. He didn't stop, though. Instead, he continued to carry her back through the club to Sara and Zach's office. He banged on the door.

"What?" That from Zach. At the moment, he probably had his dick so far inside Sara she could taste him in the back of her throat. But Conall didn't care.

"It's Conall."

"Hold on."

Normally he'd never interrupt the two of them, pretty much because he liked not having his throat torn out. But this was different. After three minutes, the door opened. A sweaty Zach glaring at them. He could smell Sara all over the man.

But Zach took one look at Conall's face and Miki's arm and stepped back, letting them in.

Sara was just zipping her jeans up when she saw Miki. "What's going on, Mik?"

"This asshole won't get his hands off me!"

He released her, letting her drop to the floor. She had to grab his arm to stop herself from falling on her ass. "Someone attacked her."

Sara walked over to Miki and stared at her arm. "Gudrun?"

"No," Conall answered before Miki had the chance. That earned him a glare.

Sara took Miki to the couch. "Sit down. Zach, in the drawer."

"Yeah. I got it."

Sara looked at her friend. "Okay, girl. What the fuck happened?"

"She got grabbed," Conall answered for her.

Miki glared at him. "I can talk for myself. They didn't rip my tongue out."

"More's the pity," Zach muttered as he stood over her with a first-aid kit. She would have been angry but she realized that, in his own Zach way, he was teasing. She grudgingly appreciated his attempt to make her feel better and diffuse the obvious tension between her and Conall.

"I needed to use my phone and reception sucks on this block. So I went down the street a bit. It was when I was coming back I heard them calling to me from the alley."

Zach frowned. "They called to you? They knew your name?"

She nodded.

"You went into the alley?" Conall barked.

Miki glared at him. "Yeah. I said, let's go see what's in the dark, scary alley all by myself. Because I'm stupid like that."

Conall growled and turned away from her.

"So what did happen?" It was starting to concern Miki that

Zach was the rational one in this conversation.

"This person grabbed my arm. So I handled it."

Zach and Conall frowned as they looked at her, but Sara smiled.

"Is there blood on your Docs?"

"Nah. But I did my best to shove balls through roof of mouth." *If the she-male had balls.*

Sara gave her a thumbs-up, then proceeded to clean off her wound.

"Was there only one?"

"I don't think so. There were more in the alley."

Conall growled again, but she didn't have time to react because her best friend was sniffing her.

"What's that smell?" Sara asked, taking a couple more sniffs off Miki. "Besides blood."

Miki pulled away from her. "Dude, you're freakin' me out. I wish everybody would stop fuckin' sniffin' me!"

"Don't know. But that's what was in our territory," Conall offered.

Sara gently held Miki's wounded arm. "Were they Pride, Mik?"

"I don't know."

"They weren't Pride." Zach leaned against the desk Miki was almost positive he'd just been fucking Sara on. *Horny dogs.* "That scent is definitely not Pride."

"So then we have another player in the game. Just great."

Miki frowned as Conall suddenly started pacing. He looked like a dog trapped in one of those kennels. She expected him to start barking and running in circles or start chewing at his leg.

"Well, luckily this isn't that bad or that deep." Sara smiled.

"It could have been a lot worse."

"I know."

"Any chance I could talk you into delaying going to Seattle?"

Miki knew this was coming, and why she originally had no intention of telling Sara anything. "No. There isn't."

Sara covered the wound with Neosporin and a bandage. "Then can I strongly suggest—"

"I'm coming with you."

Miki and Sara looked up, startled. Even Zach stood a little straighter and stared at Conall.

Miki shook her head. "I appreciate the offer, Conall. But no. That's okay. Thanks anyway."

Conall looked at her like she'd lost her mind. "I'm not asking you."

She heard Sara sigh as Miki felt the blood rushing to her brain. She tried for calm. "I don't care if you're asking me or not. I'm politely turning you down."

"I'm going. It isn't up for discussion."

She glared at Conall while Sara finished up the bandage on her arm. "Perhaps you didn't hear me clearly."

"No. I heard you. And I'm ignoring you. I'm going. So get the fuck over it."

Sara cleared her throat. "I need you to move your fingers."

"What? Why?"

"I need to make sure the bandage isn't too tight."

Miki lifted her hand up and gave Conall the finger.

"Well, that works." Sara leaned back on the couch.

"I don't need a babysitter, Conall. And I especially don't need you."

"You're not going anywhere without me. Not until we know what's going on."

"Back off."

"No."

Miki stood and walked to Conall. She stared up at him. "You so don't want to play this game with me, Viking. You just don't have the brains for it."

Well that hurt. Of course, he wasn't being rational. He was egging her on. But goddammit. Seeing her in pain. Knowing they touched her. That they could have killed her. As it was, he could barely hold the wolf in. The wolf that wanted to start tearing through the streets looking for the assholes who did this to her. The wolf that wanted to drag her back to his den and keep her safe forever.

But none of that would happen. Whatever attacked her was long gone and Miki wasn't letting him drag her anywhere now. He still couldn't believe she let him get away with it this long.

Conall leaned down, his face inches from Miki's. "Bring it on, sweets. I'm more than ready for you."

They stared at each other for at least a full minute. Then, with a snarl, Miki stalked off. She opened the door, but Conall's voice stopped her.

"Maybe I wasn't clear. You're not going anywhere without me. And that starts now."

Miki glared at him. Then she slapped her leg. "Well come on, boy! Come on. Time for your walk." She stormed out the door. "And don't forget your leash!"

Out of the corner of his eye, he saw Zach wince. But Conall didn't flinch.

Sara stared at him from the couch. "You know, you could

have just *asked* her if you could come along."

Of course, he hadn't actually thought of that as an option.

Sara shook her head. "Asshole."

℘

Miki stared at the pathetic excuse of a dog watching her from the foot of her temporary bed. "All right. If you must."

The beast clamored on top of her bed and settled in at her feet. She'd never had a dog before. She'd always left that up to Sara. Yet, especially in the mood she was in, she found him quite comforting. Considering what Sara had to live with when her grandmother was still alive, she wasn't surprised her friend always made sure to have a dog. And she understood why her heart went out to the abused, the deformed, and the freakish of the breed.

She turned the light off and settled in. Her anger had tired her out and she would probably get a few hours sleep. Good. She didn't sleep often, but she was glad when she did. A welcome respite from her brain.

She felt the dog jump down from the bed. "Hey, Roscoe. Where ya goin'?" She thought he'd spend the night. Keep her company. "Oh, whatever." She settled back down and was just drifting off to sleep when she felt Roscoe return. He jumped up on the bed and settled down right behind her. His snout against her ear, his furry forearm across her waist.

"Watch the wet snout, beast." Then she was asleep. Oddly comforted by Sara's freak dog.

Conall nudged Miki's door open with his muzzle and walked out into the hallway. He had a couple of hours before they had to leave for the airport and Miki's alarm would go off soon.

Zach was heading back to his and Sara's bedroom with two bottles of water when he stopped to intently watch Conall in that way only predators had.

"Have you no shame?" he finally asked.

Conall shifted and quietly closed Miki's door. He shrugged and smiled. "Not when it comes to her. No."

"You better be careful. That woman's deranged. And mean."

"Zach," Sara called from their bedroom, "get your tight ass back in here!"

Conall crossed his arms in front of his chest. "Yes, O great leader. And yours is so stable."

Zach snorted. "At least *I'm* getting laid."

With that, Zach disappeared back into his bedroom.

"Asshole."

He glanced back at Miki's door. It felt nice sleeping beside her. Even as wolf. She talked in her sleep. She kept spouting equations and formulas. She'd just bark them out of nowhere. Kind of entertaining, in its own twisted way.

Conall smiled. She'd get over this little anger thing eventually. See that he was trying to do what was best for her.

Hell, how mad could she be?

Chapter Eight

So far, it had been the longest day in his recent memory. From when Miki "accidentally" spit Cheerios at him during breakfast. To when she "accidentally" told the airport cops he was carrying heroin. To when she "accidentally" told the check-in staff at the hotel she was only thirteen and that Conall was her pimp. Oh, and that she was planning to bring a few "johns" into their four-star hotel. Would that be okay?

And no matter how much he wanted to wring her neck, he wouldn't. Even though she made him friggin' nuts, he'd be damned if he let her see she was getting to him.

Although she was getting to him. And not in the way she wanted to either. If anything, he wanted her more. He liked that she didn't take shit from anybody, especially him. He liked that she was mean as a snake when provoked. He liked how she smelled when pissed off.

And she was royally pissed off.

He wondered how much longer she could be mad at him. A day? A year? A lifetime? He wouldn't put it past her. He sensed the girl could hold a grudge.

Conall pulled a pillow over his head and tried to think about anything or anyone other than Miki Kendrick.

That lasted all of five minutes. Then he started obsessing over how hot she was.

Just a dog with a bone.

Well, she had to eat sometime. And except for the Cheerios, half of which ended up on the first T-shirt he wore that morning, she hadn't eaten a thing. She'd even passed on the airplane peanuts.

He threw the pillow off and went to the door that connected the rooms. He took a deep breath and knocked.

"What?"

The fact she answered him at all was a darn good sign.

Conall pushed the door open. He'd made it clear she better not lock it. If anything happened he needed to get to her. Of course, around that time the heroin incident came up. Thank Loki he had connections in the police department; otherwise, he would have endured a very unpleasant experience with a man wearing a surgical glove.

As always, she was on her laptop again. Her wounded arm, unbandaged and already healing, did not prevent her from hours and hours of typing. She'd been on that thing since they'd arrived at the airport back home. He was surprised the fucking thing hadn't fused with her body.

"Hungry?"

"No."

He took in a breath to control his desire to wring her neck and gazed around the room. She hadn't really unpacked. She just had her suitcase open, clothes already lying around. A messy girl, his Miki. He did notice the garment bag she'd hung up. He assumed those were her clothes for her meeting. Underneath them were two pairs of pumps. Both black. One had heels that were about four inches high, the other five inches.

He looked away. He had to look away. If he started

imagining those great legs of hers wearing those shoes, he would do something really stupid.

"You gotta eat, Mik...and don't throw anything at me." He could tell she was looking for something to chuck at him.

"Fine. I'll eat."

"Good. I'll order something in. We'll eat together."

"I don't want—"

"Must you argue every fuckin' thing with me?"

"Fine. Whatever. Let me know when it's here."

She went back to her laptop and it was like he no longer existed on her planet.

A rabid dog. Her own personal Cujo. Constantly lurking around. Constantly watching her. He was driving her nuts.

Still so pissed she couldn't see straight, she felt like he'd taken over her life. He was the big wolf and he was going to take care of the weak human female. She would have punched him in the stomach, but one look at that body and she knew she'd only hurt her hand.

Of course, if she had her brass knuckles...

Sara had thrown that "big ol' bear" theory at her again before Miki left with him for the airport. "He only wants to protect you."

Were these people blind? Could they not see past those rugged good looks, innocent smile and rock-hard ass? Clearly not. Clearly, she was the only one who could see him as the predator he truly was. He was the wolf and she was the cottontail just trying to make it back to her burrow—unsoiled.

Not easy when he smelled so good. Looked so good. God, did he look good. Miki didn't understand this. She'd believed herself immune to any man's charms.

"Dead below the waist" was how her last boyfriend put it. At the time, the insult had been devastating. She didn't cry about it, mostly because she didn't cry about anything. But Sara and Angie knew something was up and they quickly dragged it out of her. She should have known their answering silence was not a good thing. When the guy woke up with no body hair and his penis glued to his stomach, Miki didn't ask questions. She merely pointed the cops assigned to the case to the bar full of bikers she'd been serving that night and comfortably settled down to a life of computers and Mr. Happy for those rare occasions when she felt an overwhelming need.

Then Conall kissed her that last night Sara's Pack was in town. Suddenly, Mr. Happy was racing through an enormous amount of batteries, and when she slept, her fingers were getting quite the workout.

It wasn't fair really. Why couldn't she have this reaction to a nice guy? Not a predator *pretending* to be a nice guy. What more could she be to him anyway, other than a challenge?

Well, he'd started this. He thought he could treat her like one of those vapid whores he fucked who couldn't think for themselves. But everybody knows or should know—you never mess with a woman from Texas.

Two hours and a crap load of Italian food later, Conall was starting to feel a whole lot better. She didn't make it easy, though. But he found a way in. He screwed up facts. It absolutely drove her nuts. So he did it often. First about politics. Then about stuff Sara had told him about the three friends growing up together. Before she knew it, Miki was talking to him and beginning to relax.

Then she started asking him questions. She asked about his family. About Pack life. About Zach and Sara. And a lot of questions about being wolf. What did it feel like to change? What was different when he changed?

She had to be the most curious female he'd ever met. Constantly thinking. Constantly analyzing. He wondered what it was like in her head since it seemed like there was non-stop activity.

He also asked her questions about herself. He liked hearing her talk. Hearing her views on the world. And she had many. She also mentioned something about a photographic memory and being in one of those high IQ clubs until rude behavior got her tossed out. Not surprising. The woman was amazingly blunt. There were very few things she wouldn't say.

It was late. Almost midnight. They'd finished eating and were now sitting at the small table in his room. Miki'd leaned back and put her feet up on his chair, right by his thigh. She wore her Doc Martens and white sweat socks with baggy black shorts and an army green T-shirt. He loved it when she wore shorts. He loved her legs. While they talked, he began to run his hands along her calves and he took it as a good sign she didn't slug him.

"So what you're telling me is you're kind of a hacker?"

"No. No. I *was* kind of a hacker. But that is long behind me. I'm a nice, respectable girl now. As soon as I get my doctorate, my life is going to start really rolling."

"So what did you do?"

She shrugged. "Moved some stuff around. Infiltrated a few..." she sighed, "...government organizations."

Conall raised his eyebrows. He couldn't help himself.

"But," she quickly added, "I never stole anything."

"Is that why you didn't do any hard time?"

"Well, that and my age. Thankfully, they expunged my

record when I turned eighteen. But let me tell you, no computer for three years. To somebody like me that *is* hard time.

"But you know," she continued. "It was always about the hack. It was about proving we could do it. It was always about that. Not money or stealing anything from anybody." She shook her head. "But those days are over for me. No more hacking. In fact, no activity that can get me arrested."

"That's always a good plan."

She smiled then and he immediately got hard. It amazed him really. Almost like she'd stroked him. She had both her legs on one side of him, so he took one and pulled it over so that her legs boxed him in.

"Having fun with my legs there, Viking?"

"Yup."

He stroked her legs and stared at her. She looked away once and then, after a deep breath, looked back at him. He ran his fingers lightly along her calves and across her knees. He could hear her breathing change. Hear her heart beating faster.

"Conall?"

"Miki?"

"Don't get any ideas. As it is, I'm still pissed."

"Anger can be quite the aphrodisiac."

She laughed. "Men are so pathetic. They will come up with any bullshit to get laid."

"Do you want me to stop?" He massaged the muscles in her calves.

"What if I do?"

Conall stopped and pulled his hands away. "Then I stop."

Miki rubbed her neck and stared up at the ceiling. She tried to look unaffected, but he wasn't buying it for a second.

Especially when she said, "I didn't say you *had* to stop. I just asked what would happen if I did ask you to."

"So do you want me to start again?"

Miki shrugged in response.

"That's not an answer, Mik."

She locked eyes with him. "Don't try and bulldoze me, Viking."

"I wouldn't dare."

He leaned forward in his chair and ran his hand on the inside of her thigh. "How about you tell me if you want me to stop."

"I bet you're praying I temporarily lose my powers of speech."

"Only for a few hours."

She smiled again and shook her head. When she smiled her whole face lit up and he couldn't take his eyes off her.

"God, Miki. You're so beautiful."

That seemed to surprise her. "Okay."

He stroked his hand up her thigh and inside her baggy shorts; he felt gooseflesh break out over her soft skin. "Don't you believe me?" His hand played along the very edge of her panties. *Lace. Yum.*

"It's not that I don't believe you. But it's all perception, isn't it? One man's beauty is another man's coyote ugly. I mean, it's all about society's views and—"

"Miki?"

"Yeah?"

"Stop thinking."

"That's a cute idea and all, but I don't think I'm actually capable of...of...oh God." Her hands gripped the arms of her chair as his fingers slid past her panties and his middle finger slid inside of her.

"You were saying?"

Miki tried to stay in control. Tried to keep her wits about her. But with his finger slowly stroking in and out and his eyes never leaving her face, that started to become a freakin' impossibility. "What?" He'd asked her something and for the life of her she couldn't remember what. Her with the fuckin' photographic memory.

"You were just giving me your theory on beauty and society. Thought you could finish that thesis for me."

"Um...yeah. Sure." *Okay, Kendrick. Focus. Focus. You can do this. He's just testing you. Oh, my God in heaven, that feels so freakin' good!* "You see, it has a lot to do with...um..."

"A lot to do with...what?"

"Well, society and...uh...people..." She closed her eyes. "They are raised to...um...see..." She gripped the arms of the chair harder and wondered if she might just rip the fucking things off.

"See what?" He slid another finger inside of her and let his thumb brush her clit.

She almost came out of her chair with that. Instead she let her head fall back. Her breath coming out in short, hard gasps. "Uh..."

"Miki?"

Okay. He won. She couldn't think of one goddamn thing at the moment. Nothing but him and that big talented hand of his. Unable to stop herself, she moaned out, "Oh God, Conall."

She got the feeling that was what he'd been waiting for. Conall slid off his chair and kneeled in front of her. Leaning forward, he brought his mouth to her breast and sucked on it through her T-shirt. She gasped and wrapped one of her hands in his thick hair, pushing him forward so he could get a better grip on her nipple. And she had been right. His hair did feel like silk against her skin.

Shit. This had so not been a part of her plan. At all! But then he'd started touching her and she couldn't believe how much she loved it. Nothing had ever felt that good before. Now with Mr. Happy more than twenty-three-hundred miles away, she was about to come without him. She never had before, but Conall was bringing her there. Her own live Mr. Happy.

Closing her eyes as the sensations began to build inside her, Miki brought her other hand up and gripped the back of Conall's neck. She pulled him tight against her, his fingers continuing to move inside her. He brought his mouth to her other breast and sucked on the nipple until that was rock hard. Then he moved his tongue across her collarbone and up one side of her neck. She felt heat spreading throughout her body as Conall whispered in her ear, "You smell so good, Miki. Feel so good. I could stay inside you forever."

That was the last bit she needed. Her orgasm burst inside her and she clung to Conall, his thumb rubbed against her clit, drawing out her release until she screamed against his neck.

When Miki's vision cleared, she realized she still held onto him. "Conall?"

"It's okay, baby. I've got you." His hand slipped out of her and he picked her up, walking over to the bed. He dropped them both to the mattress, rolling on top of her, kissing her neck, her jaw.

"Conall?"

He pulled away and looked down at her. "You really are beautiful, Miki."

"Thanks, Conall."

He stared at her a moment longer. Smiled. Then passed out.

Suddenly the biggest guy she'd ever met had her pinned to the mattress. *A really ugly way to die.* She pushed the thought away and dragged herself out from under him. Luckily, he hadn't fallen completely on top of her. It seemed like at the last minute he moved over enough to crash more to her side.

Miki dropped to the floor. *Well, that had been interesting.* She took a deep breath to calm her body down. She was still rolling from that orgasm, but she wasn't going to let that distract her. And she wasn't going to feel guilty either. He'd started this game, was it her fault he'd underestimated her?

She stood up and looked at her watch. Her calculations had only been three minutes off. Not bad. She had to guess the time he'd finally drop based on what Sara had told her about their metabolisms. Thank goodness for Pharmacology 101. Best three credits she ever earned.

She went back to her room and changed into clothes that didn't have Conall's smell all over them. Then returned to her oversized shapeshifter in his bedroom. She looked down at him and realized that asleep he did look like the innocent teddy bear everybody kept talking about.

She checked his pulse and his pupils. He was out cold, but breathing normally. She made sure his body lay in a comfortable position, brushed his blond hair out of his face, grabbed her backpack and snuck out the door.

Chapter Nine

Miki sat with the closest friends she had outside of Sara and Angelina, and realized that after all these years they were still a bad influence.

"You still have Feds coming to your door and yet we sit here hacking into a man's computer?" she growled.

Craig grinned, but never looked away from the laptop he diligently worked on. "Yeah. They're like friends now. I make them coffee."

Miki shook her head. "You're nuts."

"Dude, they have nothing on us. They're just fishing."

Miki put down her Shirley Temple. "But you guys are hacking into someone's computer. So you're giving them ammunition." Miki ate pretzels out of a bowl then briefly obsessed over how many hands had actually been there before her. "Who are you going after anyway?"

"Mitchell Leucrotta."

Miki frowned. "Who?"

Her four friends stared at her. All scrunched together in the booth opposite her, they leaned on top of one another trying to see what Craig was doing on the laptop.

Amy glanced at Craig. "*Professor* Mitchell Leucrotta."

Miki groaned. "Are you guys nuts? Have you lost what little bit of your minds you have left?" Hacking into another university was dumb. Hacking into your own was damn suicidal career-wise. And the thought of Craig being the butt buddy of someone in prison was simply not a pleasant thought.

"I'm almost positive he's holding up my grant money." Craig, like her, still worked on his dissertation. Yet he had his own lab in the biotech school and would probably be a very rich man one day. If he didn't have a weird fetish about feet, she would have dated Craig herself. But, as it was, they were better off as good but strange friends.

"Whatever you find, you can't use it against him. Not legally." Miki shifted around in her seat and Craig stared at her.

"You so want to see what we're doing, don't you?"

Miki turned her head away. "No."

"Liar." Amy Bitter, who loved her name, accused. Amy could take apart and rebuild absolutely anything no matter how complex.

"You want to touch the keyboard. You lust for the keyboard." That from Kenny Liu. A software genius who loved creating viruses.

"You're all idiots."

Ben Klein, whose hacking skills made hers look like child's play, raised an eyebrow. "She desires the keyboard as much as she desires to help us with the password."

"I'm not listening." Miki put her hands over her ears. "You can't lead me down this road of evil and prison time."

"This is part of your 'I'm a good girl now' plan, isn't it?" Amy asked sweetly.

Miki took her hands away from her ears. "Yup. I'm a very good girl."

Craig grimaced. "Don't say that."

"Why?"

"Because to guys it just means you swallow."

"Grow up," Miki snapped while trying not to laugh. "How about, I'm going to be a very respectable girl with a life."

"We have lives." Kenny grabbed his bottle of ale off the table. "Sad, lonely, bitter lives. But lives just the same."

"But what about our plan to rule the world, Miki? Or at least Microsoft?" Ben pushed his empty bottle of ale away. "You and me. We had big dreams."

"You guys are boneheads." Yet she loved each and every one of them. She connected with all of them in junior high through an online game before online games were hot. Together they'd begun a minor reign of terror against big corporations. But Miki was the only one busted. She never turned them in, even though she could have gotten off scot-free by turning state's evidence. Because of that they were loyal to her. She knew it was no accident they all ended up attending the same university.

"Okay. Let me make this clear. I'm here for one reason. To get my doctorate and to get a life. Sara and Angelina are passing me by. I don't want to wake up forty, still living in Texas, alone and bitter. So, until further notice, I will not be doing anything remotely..." she cleared her throat, "...illegal."

She didn't know what expression she had on her face, but Amy was all over it.

"Except that you've already done something illegal."

"What? No."

Amy leaned forward. "Bullshit, Kendrick. Come on. Tell us. You'll feel better. What was it? Corporate espionage? Credit card theft? Identity theft?"

Miki stared. "The fact that you would think for a second I would ever do that bugs me." Then she shrugged. "I kind of drugged a man."

"Did you kill him?"

"*No*! What is it with you guys?"

"We're bored," Kenny Liu answered.

"Clearly."

"So did you just do this or...?"

She glanced at her watch. "About two and a half hours ago, give or take. Of course, that's when he reacted to it. The actual ingestion of the drug—"

"Miki," Amy cut her off. "Who the hell did you drug?"

"Just this guy. He's an...associate of Sara's." She'd filled them in months ago about Sara's new life, but she gave only the barest of details. To her friends it sounded like Sara had hooked up with this cool biker guy and ran off to live happily ever after in Northern California. Left out was anything about shapeshifters, Packs, Prides, or vicious battles in Sara's front yard. "He insisted on coming with me so he could be my big male protector."

"How did you do it?" Craig didn't even look up from the keyboard. Miki drugging someone didn't even warrant a glance.

"I combined a few things. All tasteless. Quite effective. He went to get ice and I put it in his pasta. It took about an hour or so to become active in his system. Then he went out like a light." *But not before making me scream like a little whore.*

Amy looked at Miki over her bottle of ale. "Is he cute?"

Oh, God, yes. "He's okay."

"Got a picture?"

"Maybe." Miki grabbed her backpack and dug around until she pulled out a battered picture Sara sent her five months ago.

It was a shot of the Pack with Sara and Zach in front. She knew Sara sent it to her so Miki would know she was okay.

"Here." She handed the picture to Amy. "He's the big blond one in the back."

Amy looked at the picture while Kenny looked over her shoulder. He frowned and gawked at the photo in awe. "Jesus, Miki, is this guy standing on a ladder or something?"

"And you're here why?" Amy demanded, incredulous.

"What?"

Her two friends looked up at her, but Amy spoke. "Come on, Mik. This guy is hot."

Kenny shrugged. "I'm annoyingly straight, and I think this guy is hot. Freakishly large, but hot."

"He's a pain in the ass."

"This guy?" Amy sounded unconvinced. "He looks like a—"

"If you say teddy bear, I'm going to kick the living shit out of you."

"I was going to say he looks like a sweetie."

"Well, he's not. Far from it, in fact."

"You're an idiot. I'd be on this guy in two seconds." And she would, too. Amy was a geek, but she was a horny little minx.

"I need safe and boring. He's so not that." *Amazing at hand jobs, though.*

"Why would you want safe and boring?"

"Because safe and boring gets you tenure."

"And let me guess who your idea of the perfect safe and boring guy is."

"You don't have to guess. It's Troy. Perfectly suited for me." Her friends groaned in disgust. "What? What's wrong with Troy?"

Amy sneered, "Dude, he's seriously boring. And a bit of an idiot if you ask me."

"No. No. He's just brilliant."

"Miki, he's plain ol' smart. You're brilliant. And he could never deal with that. *Ever.*"

Ben took his empty beer bottle and spun it. "I've talked to the guy. He could never deal with a woman who is smarter than he is. And you are definitely smarter than he is."

She didn't want to hear this. She'd already set Troy up in her mind as her "ideal". She didn't want to hear that he couldn't handle her. She was, in fact, hoping to meet up with him again while in Seattle. Another reason she didn't want Conall's tight ass with her.

"You guys are just snobs. Someone has to be dangerously unstable for you to find them remotely interesting."

"You mean, like you?"

Miki gave Kenny the finger.

"So, your 'new life' as you call it. What does that mean for us?" Craig again did not look at her as he plugged away on his laptop.

Miki frowned. "What are you talking about?"

"Are we still going to be compadres? Or are you going to dump our collective ass so you can hang around Troy's elitist prick friends?"

Miki was kind of hurt. "I'd never do that to you guys."

Amy motioned to the waitress for another ale. "Well, all this talk about changing your life—"

"I would never do that to you guys. Period. End of story. Understand?"

Her friends smiled, almost in relief. Miki had no idea they'd been worried.

"So, isn't this big scary guy gonna be kind of pissed you drugged him?" Ben spun his bottle again. When it pointed at Amy he leered and wiggled his eyebrows. In response she chucked pretzels in his face.

"I have it all calculated out. I have like six more hours before he wakes up. And when he does, I'm already sitting there like he simply fell asleep."

"Personally, I think he should wake up with you under him."

Miki rolled her eyes. "God, Amy. You're a horny dog."

"And yet I feel no shame."

Craig frowned at his computer. "Christ, this guy has a twenty-digit password to his freakin' email."

Amy raised an eyebrow. "It makes you wonder what he's hiding."

Miki glanced at her watch. It would be "last call" soon, but her friends wanted her to go with them to have an early-morning breakfast. Part of her wanted to go. She could use a good omelet. The other part wanted to get back to Conall. And that bugged the shit out of her. "Who is he anyway? Professor Leucrotta."

"He's new in the department. Been there about nine months or so. Surprised you never heard of him."

Miki looked up from her empty glass. "Why?"

"He fought Conridge for you. He wanted to take over your thesis and she pulled rank on him."

Miki felt fear lace up her spine. "What? Why?"

Kenny shrugged. "No idea. But he's been asking a lot of questions about you."

A look of panic crossed Craig's face. "Maybe he's a cop."

Miki could only hope.

ೞ

Miki rubbed her tired eyes and leaned back into the driver's seat of the SUV. She hated driving the fucking thing. She'd rather have a cute little sports car. Something that fit her height a hell of a lot better than The Boat, as she now called it. But Conall wasn't going to fit into anything tiny. He would always need to drive that big body around in trucks or SUVs.

"Sara? Are you still there?"

"Yeah. I just don't know what to say."

"Tell me I shouldn't be freakin' out."

"I can't tell ya that."

Sara would never lie to her, and finding out some professor Miki had never met before was asking a lot of questions about her wasn't something that either of them would consider "not a big deal". Not right now anyway.

"Watch your ass, Mik. I want you back here with Conall as soon as you're done."

"Yeah. Not a problem."

"Well, whatever you do, keep Conall close to you. I'm serious, Mik."

"Uh...okay." Her mistake was the pause.

"What? What did you do?"

"Nothing."

"You're lying to me, Miki Kendrick." When her friends used her full name, she knew she was in trouble. When they added in her middle name, she knew she'd gone too far.

"I just went out with Craig and the guys without him, is all."

"How? He'd never leave you. I know him. So how did you get away from him?"

"Um..."

"Miki Marie Kendrick! You drugged him, didn't you?"

Miki winced. Boy, did Sara and Angelina know her well. "He'll be fine."

"You get your ass back to that hotel and you make sure he is! *Right this fuckin' minute!*"

"Okay. Okay. Calm yourself. I'm already at the hotel."

"And make sure he doesn't say anything to Zach. He barely tolerates you as it is. I don't want to have to fight my own mate every damn Thanksgiving."

৪৩

She used her keycard to get into her room, easing the door open and sliding in. She figured she still had a good hour before Conall snapped out of it, but no use stomping around and waking the man up before then. She quietly dropped her backpack to the floor and looked through the adjoining door. They'd pulled the heavy hotel curtains closed the night before so it was dark in Conall's room. She crept in, trying to make out the bed. As she got closer and her eyes became accustomed to the gloom...

Oh, shit.

"Looking for me?"

Miki squealed and spun around to see the outline of Conall's body standing behind her. She could barely see him in the dark, but she could see those glinting eyes reflecting the light from her room.

"Uh...Conall. Um...before we jump to any conclusions..."

He stepped toward her and she backed away. "You mean the conclusion that you drugged me and then ran out?"

"Yeah. That conclusion." Okay. No reason to panic. Conall wouldn't hurt her. Would he? No. Not Conall. Of course, he did look seriously pissed.

"Do you realize you could have killed me? You don't know how our bodies work. You don't know what you are doing."

"I knew enough to make a good judgment call." Of course, Conall had woken up way before he should have. So how good a judgment call could it have been?

He still came toward her and she still backed away. Now that her eyes had become accustomed to the dark, she could see exactly how pissed he was. And he was really pissed. He looked like the marauding Viking she'd been accusing him of being. "You're making 'judgment calls' about my life?"

Okay. That was a good point. She put on her soothing voice. "You know, Conall..."

"Don't try and placate me, Miki. Just don't." His voice remained calm, which made her much more nervous than if he were yelling at her.

Miki felt the back of her legs hit the bed. Conall blocked her way to the door, so she went up on the bed and over it. She stood on one side, he on the other.

Since soothing and placating didn't seem to be working, she decided to just be herself. "You started this shit. I told you to stay out of my life and you thought you could handle it. Guess you were wrong."

"You are such a little bitch."

"Oh, that's a news flash!"

His eyes narrowed and she realized they weren't merely

glinting from the light. His eyes had shifted. He was so pissed his eyes looked just like a wolf's. Probably not a good thing.

"You keep moving away from me, Mik. Why is that?"

"'Cause I'm not an idiot."

"Really?"

She figured he'd come across the bed for her. But instead, he grabbed the headboard with his left hand and with one good yank, tossed the entire bed across the room. The fact that the frame had been bolted to the wall and floor was not lost on her.

Holy shit...

Conall walked toward her, closing the space between them. She backed away until she found herself up against the wall. He moved in front of her, placing his arms on either side of her body, his palms resting flat beside her shoulders. She crossed her arms in front of her chest and glared up at him.

"What? *What!*"

"You just took this to a whole new level."

"And what's *that* supposed to mean?"

"That the gloves are off."

"Oh, I'm quaking."

His wolf eyes swept up and down her body once. But in that one gaze, it was like he'd ripped off all her clothes. To her surprise, it wasn't really an unpleasant feeling. "You will be."

"Bring it on, Viking. I do so love a challenge."

He smiled and it took all her strength not to run for her life. His incisors had extended. He had wolf eyes and fangs. So not a good thing.

"You really think you can handle me, baby?"

No. But she wasn't about to tell him that. "Already I'm bored."

With a snarl, he grabbed her by the shoulders and lifted her up against the wall. Then his mouth was on hers. It was a vicious kiss. One that drew blood when his fangs grazed against her lips. But she didn't care. Not when she was experiencing the most amazing adrenaline rush of her life.

His tongue slid into her mouth and she tasted him and her own blood. At first, she didn't know what to do. But then it was like her body had a will of its own. Her legs wrapped around his waist and her hands were under Conall's T-shirt, running over all that smooth, hard skin packed with tight muscles, and settling on those narrow hips. She felt his hands under her shirt and on her breasts, her bra torn apart in one pull.

For that moment, her friends, her dissertation, Troy, her attempts to dispute the Pythagorean Theorem, all forgotten. Instead, she couldn't think past Conall touching her. He felt so good next to her skin. She wanted to be naked and she wanted this man inside her. And it seemed Conall had the same idea. His hand reached under her short denim skirt and snatched off her panties.

She dug her fingers into his hair and groaned into his mouth as he gripped her ass tight. She was sure she felt his claws just beneath his skin, but he hadn't let them loose. Yet.

He stopped kissing her so he could attack her neck. She wondered whether he'd mark her or not. Normally, she'd fight that. She knew from Sara what it meant. But at the moment, rational thought didn't exist for her. Especially once that mouth of his moved down to her breast and she felt his fangs graze across her nipple. Her whole body jerked violently and she gripped him tighter.

Conall undid his jeans and had them and his boxers around his ankles. Miki could feel the heat from his erection as it pressed against her. She knew she should stop him. If for no other reason than to tell him to put a condom on. But she was lost. Hopelessly lost.

Then the knock on the door came. She and Conall froze.

"Hey, Miki?" Craig's voice. *Oh, shit.*

Conall growled. A low, scary one as he glared at her with accusing wolf eyes. "Who the hell's that?"

"My friend."

There was another bang at the door. This time more insistent.

Miki began to say something, but Conall's hand suddenly covered her mouth. "Not. A. Word," he bit out between clenched teeth. "Hold on," he barked at the door.

He took several deep breaths, then slowly released Miki. She slid down his legs, his erection gliding right across her flesh and she let out a little moan before she could stop herself.

"You're killing me," he whispered angrily before he pushed her away, pulled his boxers and jeans up, and went toward the door.

"Conall." He glared at her over his shoulder. "Fangs," she whispered.

He blinked, realizing parts of him were still wolf. He closed his eyes and cracked his neck. When he opened them again, his eyes were his normal blue and his fangs had receded back into normal incisors.

Miki pushed down her skirt and kicked her torn panties and bra across the room and under the bed as Conall answered the door.

"Yeah?"

"We're looking for Miki."

With a grunt, Conall stepped back, allowing Craig, Ben, and Kenny Liu to walk into the hotel room. They gawked at

Conall like the main attraction at a freak show.

"What are you guys doing here?"

Kenny was the first one who could actually tear his eyes away from Conall. "Um...you forgot something."

No she didn't. She didn't forget anything. Her friends were checking up on her. They'd probably dumped off Amy and then started wondering what would happen to Miki when Conall woke up. She thought only Sara and Angie were that protective of her.

"Oh, yeah? What?" She loved her friends, but she wasn't above giving them a hard time for the hell of it.

"Uh..." Kenny looked at Ben who looked at Craig who finally turned away from Conall to look at Miki.

"Um..." He patted his pants. "The...uh...fifty bucks I owe you." Craig pulled out his wallet and took out several bills. He walked across the room and handed them to Miki.

"That's the best you can do?" she asked quietly with a smile.

"We were desperate," he whispered back. "And should I ask what happened to the bed?"

Miki glanced at the displaced bed and back at Craig. "Earthquake."

"Miki," he whispered fiercely through his teeth. "This isn't funny. Did you know your lip was bleeding?"

Conall desperately fought to get himself under some control. He'd never lost it like that before. *Never.* This one woman had pushed the beast out of him, but she didn't run screaming like any normal person would have. Instead she'd almost fucked him.

And he almost took her. Right up against the wall. No

condom. No rational thought. No thought for consequences. He knew Miki was healthy as a horse—Sara told him often enough. He was surprised the female didn't pull out Miki's blood tests as proof. So that wasn't even an issue for him. But he also knew from looking at her she was a fertile girl. True, he wanted kids one day but right this minute? And with Miki? The woman who had drugged him and left him to go hang with her friends. Really, wasn't he just trying to get laid here?

Maybe not. Maybe he wanted more. More from the one woman the wolf in him seemed to respond to.

But Miki Kendrick taunted that wolf like it was a small Jack Russell Terrier behind a neighbor's fence. *Crazy woman.*

He watched Miki speak to the nerdy imbecile. If they had been in high school together, he would have kicked that guy's ass on a daily basis.

Of course, the way he was leaning into Miki at that very moment, Conall might still kick his ass.

Miki ran her tongue along her bottom lip and tasted her blood. Christ, things had spun out of control, hadn't they? She heard Conall growl from across the room and saw all her friends tense. She had to get them out. Now.

"I just bit my lip, it's nothin'." She turned Craig around and pushed him toward the door, both her hands against his back.

"You sure you don't need anything else?"

A box of condoms? "No. But thanks. And thanks for the fifty." Which she had every intention of keeping.

She shoved Craig out the door, then grabbed Kenny and Ben by their jackets and forced them out. "Thanks, guys. See ya!"

She closed the door on her friends and turned to face

Conall. He didn't say anything, merely stared at her.

"What?" she finally snapped.

"Who the hell were they?"

She pushed off from the door and moved across the room. "*They* are none of your business."

"Fine. Whatever." He headed to the door, snatching his biker jacket up as he walked toward it. "I'll be in the diner across the street when you're ready to go to the campus."

With a slam, he was gone.

Chapter Ten

Conall pushed his second helping of waffles away. Obviously, he was upset—he wasn't eating as much as he usually did.

Miki. Fuckin' Miki. She'd done this to him. That tricky, sadistic bitch. He couldn't wait to fuck her brains out.

He shook his head. *No. No. No.* She was a treacherous female he should stay away from. He shouldn't be burying any part of himself into any part of her. She was dangerous. Like uranium. But the way she'd moaned his name when she had that orgasm...

Okay. He was doing it again! He would not think about her and the way she moaned anything. Never again. He would never let a woman get that close to him again. No matter how cute, sexy, brilliant, or dangerously unstable she may be.

In fact, he was done with women altogether. There was absolutely nothing wrong with celibacy. A fine, admirable way to live. Hell, Gandhi did it.

"Well, hello, sunshine."

Conall glanced at the female standing next to him. She was barely taller than Miki. Another mighty-mite. Great.

"What do you want?"

"And the girls told me you were considered the nice one."

No. More like the stupid one. "What does a Pride female care about nice?"

She slid into the bench across from him. "Uh-oh. Someone looks sad." Christ, this woman was the queen of sarcasm.

"Exactly who are you?"

"Victoria Löwe."

"Of the Löwe Pride?" German lions. Great. His day just kept getting better and better.

She nodded. "And you're Conall of the Magnus Pack."

"Yeah." He didn't ask how she knew that. He didn't want to know.

"Well, Mr. Magnus—"

"It's Conall. Or Mr. Víga-Feilan if you want to be formal."

And like that, the girl's whole body language changed. He smelled the sudden waft of wariness coming off her. "You're a Víga-Feilan?"

"That's my family name. But I'm not part of that Pack. I've always been a Magnus."

She seemed to relax a bit from that, but remained wary. He didn't blame her. Einarr and his kin had made quite a name for the Víga-Feilans. Pride and Pack alike hated them. Clearly his family still bought into that Viking bullshit. Problem was they weren't floating around in long boats and decimating monasteries anymore. *Assholes.*

"So, what do you want?"

"To talk."

Conall glanced over his shoulder. There they sat. A Pride of Löwe females quietly watching them, waiting to tear him to pieces. They were what he expected from Pride. But this one, she was a bit of a runt. Maybe she had some mountain lion in her.

"And that's why you tracked me here?"

"Oh, honey, don't flatter yourself. I didn't track you anywhere. Actually, my girlfriends and I are going to the rodeo. I'm hoping to find me a cowboy. And then I saw you sitting here all by your lonesome. And one of my girls recognized you."

"Okay. Then talk."

"I heard about your Pack and the Withell Pride. Such ugly business."

He sighed. "I'm bored."

"Personally, I'd rather not have a repeat of that incident, if possible."

"And how do you propose that? By letting the Packs roll over and expose our collective bellies?"

"Dogs. I swear, everything is just so black and white with you guys. It's cute in its simplistic, puppylike way."

"You know, I've had a really bad morning, and I'm not above reaching across this table and snapping your neck like a twig."

"If you're the nice one, I'm really curious about your Alphas." She shrugged. "I heard your Alpha Female's friend got attacked at one of your clubs. I merely wanted to let you know that it wasn't us."

He knew that but, clearly, she was worried he didn't. "And you speak for all the Prides?"

She nodded. "As a matter of fact, I do."

For the first time, Conall really looked at the girl. She was beautiful and young. Maybe a little too young to be speaking for all the Prides. Still, he was willing to give her the benefit of the doubt. "So you didn't send them. Then where did they come from?"

"I have no idea."

"And I'm supposed to trust you because..."

"I'm adorable."

Conall chuckled at that. She was adorable. Dangerous and adorable.

"Am I interrupting anything?"

Maybe it was the way Miki was staring at them. Like she caught them fucking on the diner table. But whatever her look, he *did* feel guilty. But why the fuck should he feel guilty? It's not like he drugged her to go off and meet with anybody.

He looked away from her, unwilling to think too much about her and how cute she was with her hair still wet from a recent shower.

"No. No. I was just leaving." Victoria started to slide out of the booth.

"You don't have to go." Okay. Now he was just being a prick.

He heard Miki grind her teeth together. *Good.*

"Maybe she doesn't have to go. But you do. I need to get to campus."

Conall looked at Victoria. "Are we done?"

"I've said what I had to. Now I've got to get myself a cowboy." She smiled at him. "Thanks for listening, Conall. I guess you are the nice one."

She stood up and looked at Miki. "He's all yours." Then she walked back to her Pride.

He pulled his wallet out of the back of his jeans and threw money on the table. By the time he stood, Miki had already stormed out the door.

He found her by the rented SUV. He unlocked the doors and they both got in.

"Who was that?"

"Victoria Löwe." He started the vehicle and pulled out of the parking lot.

"She's Pride?"

"Yup."

"And you're sitting around chatting with her in a diner?"

"Apparently so."

They didn't speak again until they hit the campus.

As far as she was concerned, that little ten-minute trip was the longest *ever*. Conall parked as close as possible to the building she needed to get to, then he shut off the motor and stared straight ahead. Miki grabbed her backpack, ready to storm off, but his voice stopped her. "When you're done, come back here. Don't go anywhere else. Don't try and sneak off. 'Cause I will find you. And if I have to do that I'll be much less pleasant."

"You're being an asshole."

"Sorry. It must be the aftereffects of *the drugs you gave me!*"

Miki didn't even flinch when he started yelling. "You're going to hold that over my head forever, aren't you?"

Conall stared at her with his mouth open.

"What?"

He turned away from her. "Don't let the door hit you on the way out."

Okay. Fine. He wanted to be an unforgiving asshole, he could be an unforgiving asshole. *Self-righteous prick.*

She jumped out of the SUV, pulled her backpack over both her shoulders, and cut across campus toward her advisor's office.

"Hey, psychopath!" Miki, halfway to her destination, turned around to see Amy and Craig walking toward her.

"Hey."

"You okay?" Amy knew her well. "I can't tell if you're pissed or sad."

Both. "It's nothing. I'm okay. What are you guys doing up so early? Or did you even bother going to bed?"

Amy sighed. "I gotta teach a bunch of freshmen about quantum physics. Three hours of my life I'll never get back." She bitched a lot, but Amy was one of the best associate professors the university had. And if they were smart, they'd cough up and give her tenure before MIT or Harvard finally stole her away.

"And I'm here to see Professor Leucrotta." Miki felt a shudder go down her spine at Craig's muttered words. And it wasn't one of those cool ones Conall gave her. But one of those creepy shudders she got like when she saw a spider crawling around her bathtub.

"Why?"

"Don't worry. He agreed to meet with me about the grant money. Maybe I'll be able to track down his password while I'm in his office."

"Be careful. Don't do anything stupid."

"Who? Me? And where is my fifty bucks?"

She smirked. "I believe you *forgot* to give me that this morning."

"You're not giving that back to me, are you?"

Miki grinned. "Nope. But thanks for checking up on me."

"Anytime. We felt like we couldn't leave you alone with Conan the Barbarian."

"Hey, Mik." Amy nudged her. "Check it out. Your boring dream man." Miki followed Amy's nod and saw Troy Benson walking toward her.

"Miki? Is that you?"

Miki braved a smile at Troy and quickly slipped her backpack off her shoulders. Nothing geekier than walking around with a giant backpack attached to you. And Troy was so not geeky. Almost six feet tall—a nice *normal* height, unlike some other abnormally large males she knew—with light brown hair and dark green eyes. She'd had a crush on him since Advanced Chem. Not surprisingly, Troy had his arm around some tall, blonde babe who looked like she didn't eat without throwing up after, but he kissed her on the cheek and sent her on her way before walking over.

"Wow, you haven't changed. Still my little Miki."

Funny, that didn't seem like much of a compliment.

ಹಿ

"Did she say anything else?"

Conall leaned against the passenger door of the SUV, his cell phone against his ear, and stared out at the deserted campus. It was still early and students were just starting to appear. "Said she was trying to get herself a cowboy."

"I don't really think that's helpful."

Conall grunted and Zach was silent for a moment on the other end. "Is everything okay with you?" he finally asked.

"Yeah. Why?"

"I've just never heard you sound so much...like me."

Conall chuckled. "I'm fine."

"Miki still giving you a hard time?"

"Something like that." He wasn't about to admit to his Alpha Male he let some crazy woman drug him and take off in the middle of the night. If for no other reason, he knew Zach would never let him live it down.

"I'm sure she'll get over it eventually. Anyway, did you believe her?" *Yes!* But he was never going to believe short, vicious women again. Especially ones whose whole bodies shook during orgasm.

"Who?"

"Victoria Löwe."

"Oh...uh...yeah, yeah. I did. I believed her."

"Okay. Well, you two be careful anyway. Soon as Miki's done, bring her ass back here before my mate forces me to start drinking. When she's stressed, she paces. It's driving me nuts."

Conall sniffed the wind coming from the direction Miki had headed. He smelled something. Miki's scent, but mixed with something else. Something...male.

Conall growled.

"Conall? Are you listening to me?"

"Yeah. Sure. We'll be careful. Gotta go." He shut off the phone and followed.

ꝏ

"So? Still living in Texas, huh?"

Miki took a deep breath. She would stay calm. She could do this. Although it wasn't like Miki was exactly Miss Smooth with the moves. In fact, she could be kind of a doofus with men...except Conall. With him she didn't seem to have any problems wrapping her legs around his waist while he slammed her against a wall.

"For now. I'm going to be finishing my doctorate this week. And Conridge mentioned an assistant professor position."

"That would mean we'd be working together. Not bad. And Conridge is tough." Boy, was she. Professor Conridge was notorious throughout the university. People feared her. When Miki decided to finally finish up her thesis, her old advisor had gone to another university and Conridge volunteered to take her on. To this day, she had no idea why. She thought the woman hated her. Of course, she seemed to hate everybody.

"So that'll be great for you, huh?"

She should have noticed the look of fear on Craig's face and the look of lust on Amy's. She should have noticed the fact that the most enormous shadow had just fallen over her. But all she'd noticed was Troy and her lame attempt to get him to notice her. "Well, you know, it's definitely time for a change." She stopped talking because Troy had obviously stopped listening. Moments from turning to see what horror stood behind her since that seemed to have everybody's interest, Miki instead froze as big long arms suddenly wrapped around her and she wasn't going anywhere.

"Hey, baby." Warm lips pressed against her ear, sending a delicious and treacherous tingle down her spine and straight to her clit. "I thought you were going to see your professor. You're going to be late."

She looked up to see Conall holding on to her. He smiled. An evil wolf smile. The kind they gave just before they took down a deer.

Sonofabitch!

"What the hell—"

He squeezed her tight and Miki fought just to breathe. "You

117

always have to make sure Miki's doing what she needs to do otherwise she gets totally lost."

Miki looked at Craig and Amy but she could already see they were enjoying this way too much to do anything about it.

Conall nuzzled her neck and she thought about digging his eyes out of their sockets. "So, you going to introduce me to your friends, baby?"

Baby?

She tried to pull away, but he wasn't letting her go anywhere. And Troy looked way too freaked out by Conall to say anything. Instead he kept staring.

She would so make him pay for this later.

"No. I'm not."

Amy jumped in before Miki could start slamming her boot into Conall's instep. "I'm Amy. This is Craig. And this is Troy."

Miki stared at his neck. It was a big neck. Might spurt a lot of blood if she cut it.

"Hey, Craig. We met this morning in our hotel room."

Our?

"But it's nice to meet the other friends of my honey-bear."

Amy almost spit out her gum while Craig suddenly became interested in what was halfway across campus. Troy looked a little disappointed as he stared at Miki. She could see her future slipping away.

"Troy—" she began. But one of Conall's big hands slid under her T-shirt and suddenly she felt claws. His claws, running lightly across her stomach.

I am going to kill him.

"Baby, we better get you to your professor's office or you're going to be late. Nice meeting you, Amy. Craig. Trey."

"It's Troy."

"Whatever." Conall's hand gripped Miki's and dragged her away. She barely had a chance to grab her backpack before she was stumbling behind him.

"Which building?" he bit out.

"Fuck you!"

He suddenly pulled her into his arms. To anyone else it probably seemed affectionate, but she knew better. And, as it was, she was way too pissed to feel anything but homicidal rage anyway. He leaned in close, his hot breath in her ear. "Keep it up and I'll make you wish they'd finished you in that alley."

"That one. Over there."

Conall again started moving, pulling Miki behind him. He walked into the building, found a stairwell, and dragged her inside it. As soon as he released her hand, she slugged him in the chest. Then cursed up a blue streak when she felt the pain all the way up her arm. Of course, he didn't even flinch.

"Are you done?" he snarled.

"Sonofabitch! What the fuck was that shit!" She shook her hand out, worried she broke a knuckle. Conall suddenly caught it and rubbed the knuckles between his two hands while he glared at her. She was almost positive he didn't even realize he was doing it.

"Who the hell was that guy anyway?"

"Who? Troy?" Was he jealous? Well, then, she shouldn't disappoint. "*That* was the future Mr. Miki Kendrick."

Wrong! *He* was the future Mr. Miki Kendrick. Not some lame, tiny man with tiny little hands. He took one look at the guy and knew he was an asshole. No way would Conall let Miki anywhere near that guy. True, she was a vindictive bitch. But

119

she was *his* vindictive bitch. He knew that now. No more bullshitting around. No more debating about what he really wanted. Miki Kendrick was his.

Clearly, though, he needed new tactics. The usual wasn't working with her. Mostly because she was nuts. But he was flexible. And mean enough to go after what he wanted.

"I think you need to stay out of my life, Viking." She tried to yank her hand out of his grasp, but he wasn't letting go.

"And I think you fail to realize that I now have the upper hand here."

"What? For drugging you? You expect me to believe for a second you'd hurt me or turn me in to the cops?"

"No. But who knows what I would do to *him*."

Miki froze. Those big, beautiful brown eyes staring up at him. "You. Wouldn't. Dare."

"You spit food at me. You set me up with the cops at the airport. And you *drugged* me. Do you really want to test the 'you wouldn't dare' theory now?"

He could see the muscles of her jaw clenching and unclenching. She was so pissed off, which only made her smell so tasty.

"Leave him alone, Conall. He didn't do anything to you."

He kicked her backpack out of the way. "But what about you, Mik? Does he have you?"

"Nobody has me."

He stepped toward her until she backed herself up against the wall. He'd never worked so hard to be menacing before, but Miki kept bringing that out in him. And it didn't help that every time he did it, the smell of her lust punched him in the face.

"But I want you."

"So I gathered."

"And if I'm busy chasing you around, I can't exactly be kicking the living shit out of him, now can I?"

Miki crossed her arms in front of her chest. "I guess."

"So then maybe we make a little agreement."

"What kind of agreement?"

"You give me until Friday."

"To do what?"

He placed both his arms on the wall above her and leaned in. "To get close to you. After you defend your thesis, if I haven't gotten between those sweet thighs of yours by then, it's over. I never bother you again. I won't even look at you."

"You have got to be kidding me."

"When it comes to you, I don't joke around."

He expected her to kick him in the 'nads. But she didn't. *Interesting.*

"At least give me a shot, Mik." He gently pulled her arms away from her body and leaned in to her. She watched him closely, but didn't try and stop him either. "See? That wasn't so hard, now was it?" He leaned down and kissed her. A small one. His lips against hers. She didn't pull away, so he nipped at her bottom lip until her mouth opened and she let him in. His tongue moved slowly over hers, savoring the taste of her. She tried to pull her arms away, but he held them tight, moving them so he had them flat against the wall over her head. He pinned her with his lower body, his knee sliding in between her thighs.

She moaned and he knew he had her.

What in hell was she doing? Had she lost her mind? Was she actually making out with the Viking in the stairwell of the biotech school? This was definitely a new low. It was early, but

121

there were already professors and students everywhere. Sooner or later, they'd get caught. This was insane. She was insane. How exactly could she expect to get tenure at the school if she got caught getting all hot and bothered with some guy in the stairwell?

She needed to tell him to stop. She needed to push him away. She definitely didn't need to moan. In fact, she really had to *stop* moaning.

Conall pulled out of the kiss and leered at her. "Yeah. That's what I consider letting me get close."

If she had the strength, she would have punched him again. In fact, she was all ready to risk her knuckles just for the hell of it.

But before she could deck him, Conall kissed her cheek, stepped back, and pulled her out from under the stairs where he'd trapped her.

"Miss Kendrick. I hope I'm not interrupting anything."

Conall and Miki looked behind them and up. At the top of the stairs stood the dragon lady herself. Professor Irene Conridge. An imposing forty-ish woman, wearing one of her plain blue suits and a pair of killer fuck-me pumps. The woman had always been a total dichotomy.

"Really. I know how busy your schedule is. And as all I'm doing is running an entire department, please feel free to keep me waiting for another fifteen minutes."

Miki snatched her arms away from Conall and pushed past him. "Professor Conridge. I'm so sorry. I lost track of time..." *Because I was busy getting fondled.*

Grabbing her backpack, Miki yanked Conall's hair as she ran by, but she got the feeling he would only see that as more foreplay. She charged up the stairs, but Conridge had already walked off.

Miki stopped at the top of the stairs and looked back at Conall, hauling her way over-packed bag onto her shoulders. "I don't know how long I'll be."

"It's okay. Take your time. I'll be here." Of course he would. Because he was torturing her.

"Miss Kendrick!"

Miki shook herself out of her stupor and charged off.

Chapter Eleven

Conall sat on the stairs and worked really hard to control his raging hard-on. Man that woman was a little firecracker. It didn't take much to get her worked up. To get her hot and wet. For him. He growled and forced his wolf back on its chain.

Nope. No one else was going to be good enough for him. He wanted Miki. Not for a night. Or even a week. But for a lifetime. He would have her, too. He'd just have to convince her. And hell, how hard could that be?

Conall frowned. There was that smell. The same smell from the rave. The same smell on Miki after her attack.

This time he'd smelled it as soon as they'd moved into the stairwell, but Miki had him totally distracted. Now he couldn't ignore it.

It was faint, so he didn't think any danger was near, but still...

Conall sniffed the air and realized it came from another floor. He followed the scent, letting it lead him up one flight of stairs. He could tell Miki was on this floor. He could smell her delicious scent above all others. He went up another flight. There were several labs on this floor. He walked past them. Past a bunch of classrooms. Then he found an alcove with professor offices. He followed the scent until he reached a door. He tried the door without success. Locked. He stuck his nose right up against the wood and sniffed. Then he sniffed again. He knew that smell. He knew it from somewhere. He sniffed again. A deep long one.

Then it hit him. Right between the eyes. He couldn't believe he hadn't thought of it before.

"Hyena!" he barked out triumphantly.

Conall turned away only to come face-to-face with Craig.

"Hey."

Conall nodded. "Hey."

They stared at each other for another moment, then Conall walked off, positive the man watched him sniff the door like a bomb-detection dog that had located a nuclear weapon. He wouldn't worry about that now. He was too busy thinking about hyenas. The natural enemies of lions.

Conall never believed in coincidences and he wasn't about to start now. He remembered the professor's name on the door. "Leucrotta". He'd have to ask Miki about him.

Conridge crossed her long legs and stared down her nose at Miki. "Well, I believe you are as ready as you're ever going to be."

Of course, that was better than what she'd told other grad students—"Pass you? You're lucky I haven't killed you."

"Anything else I should do?"

"You reserved a classroom, yes?"

"Yes, ma'am."

"And you double-checked that all committee members know the time and place?"

"Yes, ma'am."

"Then, Miss Kendrick, you should be all set. Just make

sure you're ready to seriously defend your thesis. This isn't the time for you to get tongue-tied. Although I'm certain if that happens then life as we know it will cease to exist."

Miki smiled. "Yes, ma'am."

"So go get some rest and I'll see you on Friday at three-thirty."

"Yes, ma'am."

Miki stood and gathered all her papers together. She knew Conridge watched her, but she was too afraid to ask why. The woman was the true Dragon Lady.

"So, Miss Kendrick, who was that nice young fellow you were fondling on the steps?"

Miki dropped the half ream of paper that represented the last version of her thesis. Going to her knees, she quickly began to scoop the papers together. She'd worry about order later. Anything to stop this conversation. No way would she talk about the weirdness going on between her and Conall. She didn't understand it so how could she explain it to others? She especially wasn't going to explain it to Professor Conridge. Phi Beta Kappa. Rhodes Scholar. And all around bitch.

"Just a friend, ma'am." Anytime she was around Conridge, Miki felt like she was in the military. Yes, ma'am. No, ma'am. Please don't flunk me, ma'am.

"Do you get forced against walls by all your friends?" Holy shit, how much did this woman see? Or, even worse, hear?

She felt her face getting red. "We were just talking, ma'am."

"I see. To be honest, I'm amazed you could get him behind those stairs. He is a big boy. Even for Pack."

Miki had half her papers gathered together, but she dropped them on the floor again. Sitting back on her haunches, she stared up at Conridge. "I'm sorry—what?"

The woman smiled and came around to the front of her desk. She slid onto the top of it grabbing a silver picture frame and handing it to Miki.

"My husband. Niles Van Holtz. Of the Van Holtz Pack."

Miki didn't know what shocked her more. The fact that Conridge's husband was Pack? Or the fact that she actually had a husband? She gawked at the picture. The man was gorgeous, she'd give the woman that. It was a picture of Conridge, her husband and four happy-looking kids.

She blinked. "Van Holtz?" Then she frowned. "Of the Van Holtz restaurant chain?" She'd never been in one of those restaurants. You had to be as rich as God to be able to afford a side dish.

The woman rolled her eyes and smirked, seemingly embarrassed by it all. But not by the fact that her mate pissed on trees and could scratch his ear with his back leg. *That* didn't seem to faze her.

"Is that why you offered to be my supervisor?"

"Of course. I know how hard it is to be human among shifters. And I heard about your friend becoming Alpha Leader of the Magnus Pack. I also heard about your involvement in the Pride war. I'm impressed. I always knew you were smart. I never doubted that. I simply had no idea the damage you could do. You'll make him a good mate."

Miki stood up. "What? Conall? No. I'm not going to be his mate. Ever."

Conridge appeared confused. "Why ever not?"

"Because."

"Because...why?"

"Because I'm not getting that involved with him." Exactly how many times would she have to explain this to people? And why did they keep freakin' asking her?

"But you do realize he looked at you kind of the way Niles still looks at me. And, gosh, we've been together now more than twenty years." She had the warmest expression on her face and Miki realized she was seeing another side of this woman. Conridge loved the man she spoke of. A lot. Miki suddenly regretted calling her a "cocksucker" when Conridge kicked back the first draft of Miki's thesis with so many red marks the paper looked like it had a bleeding disease.

"But Conall doesn't feel that way about me."

"And you know this because you are so in tune with normal society."

Conridge was right. Miki wouldn't know normal if it came up and spit in her face. And she was starting to feel that no matter what she did or how hard she tried, she would never be normal.

"I...I..." Miki sat down Indian style on the floor, the wind knocked out of her. "I have no idea what I'm doing."

"There's nothing wrong with that. We all go through it. Even me."

"Really?" Miki had a hard time believing that. Conridge always seemed so put together.

"Of course. Do you think I *wanted* to be a wolf's mate? The man tackled me from behind and marked my back. Of course I hit him with a two-by-four. He needed eight stitches in his head."

Miki stared at her and Conridge shrugged. "He was still doing his take-what-he-wants thing. I've trained him not to do that anymore...and to roll over on command." The two women laughed and Miki wondered if she were looking at herself in another fifteen years.

Conridge adjusted her stockings. She actually had the kind with the seam down the back. Very 1940s and still very hot. "Look, Miki, what you are going through is a normal human emotion. And every once in a while, even people like you and me have those."

Miki grinned. The woman was quite a piece of work.

"You don't trust yourself yet," Conridge continued. "You don't trust your instincts. But you should. You're not just some brain with legs. You've got some nice survival skills. Wolves find that sort of thing incredibly sexy."

Miki smiled, pulling herself into a crouch so she could gather the papers together. "I guess I don't want to blow this. My life, I mean."

"You won't. You're smart. You're mean. You'll be fine."

Miki laughed and stood, her thesis in a messy pile in her arms. "Well, thanks for the pep talk."

"My pleasure. You know, my husband says I'm not good at pep talks. I think he's wrong."

Conridge pulled her office door open as Miki kicked her big, heavy backpack in front of her. It slid out the door and hit what she was almost certain was a man...or maybe a woman...it was something.

"Well, well. Is this the infamous Miki Kendrick?"

Miki glanced back at Conridge. Her professor's distaste for this person clearly written on her face. "Miki Kendrick. This is Professor Mitchell Leucrotta."

So it was a guy...sort of. The guy who'd been asking way too many questions about her. A weasely little fellow. Not quite Sara's height. Thin but well muscled. What her mother would have called a "scrapper". But there was something so predatory about him she began to wonder where the hell Conall was.

Wasn't he supposed to be protecting her or something? *Asshole.*

Miki nodded her head, but kept her distance. "Professor Leucrotta."

"Well, I'm off." He secured his computer bag on his shoulder. "I'm avoiding this little cretin student. I hate when they're needy."

Now Miki really hated the guy. She was almost positive he was talking about Craig. One of her best buds. And a helluva lot less creepy than this guy.

Leucrotta gave a less than masculine finger wave before strolling down the hallway.

Miki looked at Conridge. "I hate him."

Conridge chuckled. "You certainly do make snap decisions, don't you?"

"Am I wrong?"

The older woman shook her head. "No. You're not. He's a scumbag."

Conall appeared suddenly in the stairwell opposite where Leucrotta disappeared. He raised his nose in the air and sniffed. She realized he was casting for a scent. Conall followed his nose all the way over to Miki. He sniffed her. Then he sniffed her again. Miki got that little tingle in the back of her neck, and the next thing she knew, her pussy was wet.

Okay, when the hell did that start happening?

"What the hell are you doing?"

"Hyena," he muttered.

"Jackal," Miki shot back.

He looked at her and frowned.

She shrugged. "I thought this was word association."

Conridge snorted a laugh and Conall looked at her. He

sniffed the air again. "You smell familiar."

"I'm married to a Van Holtz." Boy, the woman said that with a lot of pride.

"Oh. Yeah, I remember. I met you once. It's nice to see you again. I'm Conall." He reached down and picked Miki's backpack up, throwing it over his shoulder.

"Why did you say hyena?"

"That's the smell I couldn't place. The scent that was on you after you were attacked. I've only dealt with them once or twice when I was a kid. A bunch of them beat the hell out of me in sixth grade." He looked at Conridge. "I was a lot smaller then."

"I see."

Conall looked at Miki and the papers in her hand. "Need some help there, slim?"

"Just a little."

Conall grabbed a handful. "Do either of you know Professor Leucrotta?"

Miki frowned. "You just missed him. Why are you asking?"

"That's where the scent was strongest. At his office door."

She sighed. "He was asking about me."

"What?"

"He wanted to be Ms. Kendrick's advisor for her dissertation," Conridge filled in helpfully. "I politely told him to go to the devil. He seemed to take that rather personally. I don't like him. But I didn't bring him into the university. The dean did. But there has been lots of activity from the hyena Clans lately."

"We hadn't noticed."

"Not surprising considering your hands were full with the

Withell Pride. Anyway, you may want to keep an eye out for them. They can be quite barbaric."

"I remember that. I mean, for little kids they were really vicious."

Conridge nodded. "Hyenas aren't as big as lions, but they make their lives a living hell. The females and the children are especially brutal. So watch your backs."

She turned to Miki. "You've got tonight and tomorrow to relax. I suggest you do that. Don't panic over this, Ms. Kendrick. You'll be fine."

"If you say so."

"I don't say so. I'm ordering it. Now go away." Conridge went back in her office and closed the door.

"You brilliant types can be awfully abrupt."

"What a ground-breaking observation." Miki headed back to the stairs, Conall right beside her. She wasn't shaking him any time soon.

Once outside, Conall took the rest of the papers from Miki. "Gimme." Since molesting her in the stairwell, he was in a much better mood.

"What's with you? Why are you so accommodating?"

"'Cause I won."

"You won what?"

"You. Me. The seduction. In the stairwell."

"I didn't fuck you in the stairwell."

"I didn't say you had to. I said I had to get between your legs by Friday." He grinned. "And I did."

Miki stopped and stared at him. "You're high. That was not the agreement."

"Yes, it was."

Miki made a fist, ready to deck him again when Craig walked up. "Hey, Mik. Can I talk to you for a sec?"

Miki wasn't done with Conall. "Can it wait?"

"Go ahead. I'm satisfied." Conall winked at her and walked off, her backpack and dissertation in his big hands.

"Asshole," she muttered after him.

"Dude, it's worse than that."

Miki looked at Craig. "What are you talking about?"

"I found him *sniffing* Leucrotta's door. Really sniffing it."

Miki sighed. *Damn shapeshifters.* They were simply not discreet.

"Don't worry about it, Craig. Besides, I've got bigger problems than his fetishes."

"Like what?"

"Everything."

Craig smiled. "That's a lot."

"I know."

"Look your dissertation isn't until Friday. So why don't you come to my house party tonight. Everybody's going to be there. You can even bring the Beastmaster if you want."

Well, at least he didn't call him teddy bear.

"I love your house parties." And she hadn't been to one in ages.

"Then come."

That would give her a little reprieve from being alone with Conall. "Okay. I'll be there."

"Cool. It starts at nine o'clock. Bring any video games." She chuckled. Techno geek parties were the best.

Craig headed off and she walked to where Conall stood.

She took a deep breath and forged ahead. "Look. Craig invited me to a house party he's throwing tonight...wanna come?"

He'd wondered if Miki would say anything about Craig's party. He could hear the dweeb invite her even though he stood a good hundred feet from them. When she asked him if he wanted to go he felt his heart swell a little. "Sure. Sounds great. I'm assuming I'll be your date."

"Well, you're assuming wrong. We're going as friends."

"Why?"

"Because you didn't win," she bit out between clenched teeth.

Conall watched her walk off, and waited ten seconds before he yelled after her, "Yes, I did!" He laughed when Miki raised her middle finger high in the air like a salute.

He was really starting to love that woman.

Chapter Twelve

Miki looked up as Conall held out her cell phone. "It's Angie."

Miki took the phone and watched Conall go back into the room, closing the glass door behind him. With the bed no longer attached to the wall, they'd been forced to change rooms. Conall had been polite enough not to mention how much he had to pay the hotel for that little "accident". But she loved the new room they had. She had a great view of Seattle and a small balcony she'd been sitting on for three hours with her feet up on the rail and her laptop right in front of her.

"Hello?"

"So how's the big, blond pooch? Has he started humping your leg yet?"

Miki didn't answer. She couldn't answer.

"Okay, Kendrick. Spit it."

"It's complicated."

"You fucked him?"

"No. Not exactly"

"What are you two up to?"

"Too much. It's getting out of control."

"Okay. Hold on."

Miki waited while it became quiet on the other end. She assumed Angelina was at work and had a customer.

"Okay. I'm back. And I've got Sara on the line."

"Oh, shit."

"All right, Mik," Sara said with way too much eagerness. "What's going on?"

Fuckin' Angelina with her three-way calling.

"This is too weird."

"We want details."

"Details about what?"

"She and Conall have been up to shenanigans," Angie tossed in.

"You fucked him?"

"No. She hasn't."

"Oooh. This is getting better and better."

Miki rubbed her forehead. "I hate both of you."

"You might as well tell us," Angie pushed.

"Or I can ask Conall. He *has* to tell me. I'm like totally in charge and everything."

Miki rolled her eyes. Sara's reign of terror. *Bonehead.* "Okay. Okay. We've gotten pretty...involved with each other. But we haven't actually done the deed."

"That was vague," Sara muttered.

"I'll put it in Sara-speak for ya, hon. He's either used his hand or his tongue to get her off, but no dicks have made an appearance."

How could she still be friends with these two idiots?

"Yum," Sara growled. "So what's the problem? It's time for you to cowboy up and break in that mustang."

"I can't believe you found a way to work 'cowboy up' into this conversation."

Angelina sighed. "See you need to go into this knowing what it is, Mik."

"Which is?"

"A booty call. The extended DVD version, but a booty call nonetheless."

"But what if—"

"No, Miki. No analyzing. No second-guessing. No obsessing."

"For once in your life just enjoy yourself," Sara practically begged.

Miki sighed. "To be honest, I don't think I know how to do that."

Sara chuckled. "Bartender-Miki knows how."

"Bartender-Miki? Is this like your Golden Retriever Sara vs. Drunk-Sara theory?"

"No. You, smartass," Sara growled.

"Bartender-Miki," Angie began, "is the one who always asks inappropriate questions and says whatever she thinks without caring about the repercussions."

"Bartender-Miki who used to set things on fire in Chem Lab because she was bored."

"Who taught herself Elvish and Klingon."

"Who faced off against my grandmother on more than one occasion."

"Who could kick guys ten times her size out of the bar when they got rowdy."

"Bartender-Miki who the FBI still refer to as 'that bitch'," Sara stated with obvious pride.

"That's the Miki we both know and love," Angie finished.

Miki blushed. Now she remembered why she was still friends with these two idiots. Because they both actually got her. And loved her in spite of it.

"But I was changing everything. I was supposed to be having a nice, normal, *respectable* life?"

"Normal? Who wants to be normal?" Sara asked in complete confusion.

"Fuck normal."

"I say fuck Conall. But in a good way."

Miki chuckled. "Would you two idiots focus."

"All right, Miki. Listen up." This from Angie. "Is Conall around somewhere?"

"Yeah. He's in the other room."

"Can you see him from where you are?"

"Yeah. Why?"

"Okay. Do me a favor. Look at Conall. But don't look at him like Miki who wants to have a respectable life—"

"We'll call her boring Miki," Sara chimed in.

"Instead look at him like Bartender-Miki."

"Okay." Miki thought about her nights bartending. Always in control, she never took any shit. She ruled Skelly's bar with a mighty fist and everyone respected her. She knew what she wanted and what she didn't and she acted accordingly. She felt like she'd knocked that Miki out for the last six months but she was awake now. Awake and looking at Conall like a prize-winning bull at an Austin auction.

Stretched out on the bed, on his stomach, watching TV; the Viking's big arms wrapped around a pillow. Her eyes dragged across every inch of that long hard body, taking in the muscles of his arms, the line of his body, how friggin' huge his feet were. And that outstanding ass. Plus, he was wearing that goddamn black bracelet again.

He seemed to feel her watching him. He looked at her and smiled. A smile that, deep down, she knew was for her and her alone. Instead of turning away, like she always did, she smiled back. And his smile actually got bigger. Then he winked and went back to the TV.

Miki sighed. "Holy shit..."

"We've been trying to tell ya." Sara laughed

"What do I do?"

"Be yourself," Angie insisted.

"Are you two high? That scares off most men."

"He's hardly most men, darlin'."

"How about you do me a favor?" Angelina asked.

Uh-oh. "What?"

"You've got, what? A couple of days until you have to do that thing, right?"

Miki crossed her eyes. "You mean my dissertation? Yeah. Just a couple of days until 'that thing'."

"Then why don't you just enjoy yourself?"

"Don't worry about work," Sara added.

"Or school."

"Or bills."

"We've got your back. We'll take care of everything. Just relax and see what happens."

It had been years since she could do that. Just relax. In fact, she was pretty sure the last time she did it, she was about fourteen. Before her mother died. Since then she'd never taken any handouts. She'd always worked for everything she had. And she realized it would be nice to have a couple of days where she didn't have to worry about anything.

"I guess I can."

Angie let out a breath. "Good."

"What's the worse that could happen?"

"But I'm not promising you two bitches anything. There's no guarantee anything will happen between me and him. I've never actually done the booty-call thing, and that's all a guy like him would want."

"You don't know that."

"And it doesn't matter if that's true," Angelina jumped in before Sara and Miki could start arguing. "The point is not to worry about it. It's your choice what you do with him, Mik. I just want you to relax and not worry."

"Think you can handle that?" Sara asked.

Miki took a deep breath. "I'll give it a shot."

He hadn't been able to stop looking at her since she'd walked out of the bathroom. It wasn't dramatic or anything. A cropped T-shirt, black denim miniskirt, and steel-toe Doc Martens. But it was the stockings. Dark, thigh-high wool ones with garters. And you could see the garters. The total punk, geek-girl outfit, but on her—it made his whole body hard.

She hadn't said much to him since Angie called. But he could tell something happened. She didn't seem unhappy or stressed or much of anything. For Miki that was pretty major because she was usually some kind of extreme. She didn't even complain he'd only gotten one room for the two of them since they had to move. He'd waited for her to bitch, but she seemed more concerned with the great view. He'd had to pay some serious cash for that, but it was worth it just to see her smile.

And he couldn't stop thinking about the look she'd given him when she was on the phone with Angie. He'd been minding his own business, trying to watch TV and not think about fucking her on the balcony when he realized she was staring at him. All he could figure was that she and Angie had been talking about him. But, for once, she didn't look mad or annoyed. In fact, she'd smiled at him. And he couldn't help but think that smile was for him and him alone.

The woman made him crazy. He wanted her so bad he was afraid his palms would start to sweat. As it was, he was having trouble keeping the wolf under control. Every time he smelled her—every time she came near him—he just wanted to bite the back of her neck and mark her as his for eternity.

They parked close to Craig's house and jumped out. As Conall came around the SUV, he found Miki crouching down, adjusting the laces on her Docs. He growled. He couldn't help it. Seeing her legs in those stockings was fucking killing him.

"I heard that." She stood up and grinned at him. "Try not to start howling during the party."

"Wearing those stockings, woman, I can't promise you anything."

She shook her head and moved toward the house. As she passed him, she grabbed hold of his wrist and dragged him behind her.

She'd touched him. The most innocent of touches, but it was the final nail in his coffin. Now he was hooked. And nothing would save him.

As soon as they walked into Craig's house, he knew that Miki was in her element. When the standing-room-only crowd saw her the entire place erupted into a chant. "Mi-ki! Mi-ki! Mi-ki!"

Vintage eighties music pumped through the enormous

standing speakers, as well as some recent tech. And there were enough high-tech geek supplies to take over the Pentagon. Everyone played games on the giant TV screens or plasma monitors or they were dancing...well, trying to dance. He realized that in her world, Miki was a great dancer. Because these people were the worst.

Of course, he was the biggest one there. Several guys were as tall or taller, but they were usually skinny. Like they hadn't eaten in days. Or extremely overweight. Like they never left their computer chairs.

Conall tried to ignore the guys hugging Miki as she made her rounds. She was being friendly. They were groping. But when any of them got out of hand, she handled them expertly. She actually twisted one guy's arm behind his back and slammed him up against the wall.

Conall loved watching her kick ass.

Miki had just finished singing "Love is a Battlefield" with five drunken skateboarders when Amy tackled her from behind.

"My best, best, best friend, Miki!"

She was toasted.

"Dudette. How much liquor did we have tonight?"

"Two beers." Then Amy began to giggle hysterically.

Just like the bartender she was, Miki pulled the bottle of ale out of Amy's hand and dragged her to the coffee pot.

"Drink coffee now. Or we're going to have to give you a cold shower." That way she could be a wet drunk.

"Maybe I like cold showers."

"I'll make Ben do it." Since Ben had been trying for about ten years to get into Amy's pants, Miki was confident she wouldn't have to "make" Ben do anything.

"Bitch. Where's the loyalty?"

Miki handed her a Styrofoam cup filled with coffee. "I have loyalty only to the Pack." Then Miki laughed at her own joke.

Amy watched her with narrowed eyes. "You're awfully perky, you know, for you."

"I'm having a good time." And she was in a good mood. Listening to Conall growl every time she moved had done wonders for her ego.

"It's that guy, huh? *Masters of the Universe*'s He-Man."

Miki had such geek friends. She'd already heard Conall referred to as Wolverine, The Punisher, Captain America and, her personal favorite, "One of those blond German guys from *Die Hard*".

"Don't be an idiot."

"Oh, come on. I'm surprised the guy didn't piss on your leg this morning when he saw you talking to Troy. And it's been quite entertaining watching him watch you. While you do your damn best to ignore him."

Kenny came up behind her. "What's going on?"

"I'm drunk and Miki's got Conan the Barbarian on her butt."

"It has been a hell of a display between you two."

"What are you talking about?" Miki snapped.

"Show her, Ken."

Kenny suddenly hugged her. A big, friendly one. Completely asexual. When he pulled away, they all looked at Conall. She could see his glare from clear across the room.

"That's what we're talking about."

"All of you are idiots," Miki mumbled.

"Deny everything. Admit nothing. Demand proof," her

friends stated in unison.

Miki gave them the finger and walked away. Seeing Conall's face had made her toes curl. This night was getting stranger and stranger.

Conall couldn't stop watching her. He liked the way she moved. He liked the way she acted with her friends. He liked her. More and more with each passing second.

"You know some in law enforcement consider watching someone that closely as stalking."

Conall looked down. Miki's three male friends surrounded him. Craig. Ben and Kenny Liu whom she always called by his entire name.

Conall crossed his arms in front of his chest. "Is that a fact?"

"Yeah," Craig continued. "You may be bigger than us."

"Freakishly bigger," Kenny Liu added.

"But we can do things to you that you can't even imagine."

Ben adjusted his backward baseball cap. "Real shame if something happened to your bank account."

"Or if you ended up on the FBI's most wanted list."

"Or if you were listed as dead."

Conall stared at the three men. He had to admit he was impressed. He didn't think they had any balls. He'd been wrong.

"So," Craig finished up, "if you hurt her, we'll make your life a living hell."

"And we'll enjoy every minute of it." Kenny Liu reached up and patted Conall on his shoulder. "Remember that, Conan."

Conall watched them walk away. True, he could tear their throats out, but he liked the fact Miki's friends felt that strongly about protecting her.

His gaze moved across the crowd and he caught sight of her again. She was playing a video game with some guy. It was one of those fighting ones. He and Zach had to stop playing those because they kept getting into real fistfights over them. Whatever Miki had done, she clearly won because she threw the game controller on the ground, brought both her arms up, and screamed "*In your face!*" Then she did a sad, but hilarious little victory dance.

Conall sighed. "Sure, Conall. Why go for a normal girl?"

He was about to hit the food table again when he smelled it. Cutting through the throng of people. It was a she and she was moving fast. He caught sight of her dark spiky hair as she pushed through the crowded living room.

He glanced over at Miki. Craig had pulled out a karaoke machine and they were dragging Miki up to the front. She'd be fine. She had her dangerously psychotic friends protecting her. He followed the spiky head outside and around the side of the house.

He grabbed her by the scruff of her neck and lifted her off the ground. "Where do you think you're going?"

She fought back, her claws coming out. He tossed her fifteen feet before she could slash him. She hit the ground and slid. Then she flipped herself over and stared at him. She was young. She'd dyed her golden hair black. But she couldn't hide those gold eyes or that Pride smell.

She hissed like a house cat and backed away from him. Conall frowned and slowed his pursuit. Any other Pride female would have gone for his throat by now. This one was running from him.

"Stay away from me!"

Conall stared at her and, for a moment, he thought she

145

might burst into tears.

"I was just here for the party. I...I don't want to fight you."

"Why aren't you with your Pride?" He looked around, expecting them to suddenly appear. Females attacking from every side.

"I'm not part of the Pride anymore."

"Why not?"

"That's none of your business." She scrambled to her feet. He sized her up. She was the alternative queen. All black clothes, silver jewelry, and deathly pale skin. And, of course, black eyeliner and shadow. A Goth chick. He could bet she didn't get along too well with some of the other Pride females.

Conall nodded. "Sorry about that. I thought—"

"I know. You thought I was going to fuck with you because you're Pack. No offense, but I could give a shit. That's not my life anymore." She wrapped her arms protectively around her body. "And maybe you shouldn't attack people without being sure they're actually trying to kill you. Asshole."

Then she headed up the street.

ॐ

Miki went to the food table and grabbed some carrots. She'd tried to go for a brownie earlier, but Conall had nearly broken her wrist getting her to drop it. That's when she knew they were Craig's "special" brownies. Having Conall around was kind of like having a drug-sniffing dog at her disposal.

Miki ate her carrots and looked around the room. At first she didn't see Conall. She felt a moment of annoyance at his absence. Then she felt a moment of annoyance at her moment of annoyance. And was even more annoyed at herself when she felt relief at seeing him come back in the room.

He walked over to her and took a carrot out of her hand. "Well, I've hit a new low."

"What happened?"

"I just beat up a little girl."

"Compared to you everyone's a little girl."

"She was Pride."

"Oh, yeah. The Goth chick with the gold eyes, right?"

"Yeah. Her. You saw her?"

"Yeah."

"Why didn't you say anything?"

Miki shrugged. "I didn't think about it. She's one of Amy's teaching assistants."

"You think and obsess about everything else but that doesn't seem like something you should tell me about?"

Miki was about to get good and pissed off, but then she realized he was right. "You're right."

Conall choked on his carrot. "What?"

She shrugged. "You're right. I should have said something."

"All right. What are you setting me up for?"

"Nothing." She would have been hurt if she hadn't drugged him once.

His eyes narrowed and she felt kind of guilty for making him so paranoid. "Really. I'm just telling you that you're right. I swear."

"You been eatin' the brownies?"

Miki rolled her eyes. "No."

"Drug the carrots?"

"No."

"Drug or eaten the Jell-O shots?"

"No. I didn't drug anybody or anything."

Conall backed slowly away from her. His eyes never leaving her face. "I'm watching you, Kendrick."

She stared at his body as he walked across the room to talk to a bunch of snowboarders.

He was watching her. She liked the sound of that.

A sloppy round of "Video Killed the Radio Star" with some guys who actually made money playing video games for a living, and Miki was ready for a break from the people and the heat of the room. She headed to the back of the house and went out on the stoop. Surprisingly dead in the back but, not surprising in Seattle, it was raining a bit. There were several couples in the trees behind Craig's house. She stared in their direction but she wasn't really paying attention. Watching other people fool around had never been very interesting for her.

She felt a presence next to her and turned with a smile to see...Troy. And just like that, her smile faded. "Oh. Hey, Troy."

"Hey, Miki." He sat down next to her on the stoop. She scooted over because he sat a little too close. "Where's your pit bull?"

It took her a moment to realize he meant Conall. "Inside. He seems to get along well with the snowboarders."

"I'm glad you're back, Miki."

She frowned at him. "Really?" She never thought the man even noticed her.

"Yes. I'm really hoping you'll take the job Conridge offers you."

"She hasn't offered me anything yet."

"She will."

Miki shrugged. "Whatever."

She stared at her boots. She had nothing to say to this man. In fact, she wanted him to go away.

"You know, Miki," his hand landed on her knee, "I've been thinking about you all day."

Miki turned to look at him and, suddenly, Troy's lips were on hers. She could taste the liquid courage he'd been guzzling to make this move, but he took her by surprise and that was always a mistake with her. She shoved him so hard he flipped off the stoop and landed in a heap.

Miki leaned over. "You okay, Troy?"

He lifted his arm. "I'm fine." But it was muffled since he went face first in the dirt. "I'm just going to lie here for awhile. Don't mind me."

Christ, how did she ever think this guy was cute or sexy? Just the touch of his lips against hers made her want to spit.

As she wiped the back of her hand across her mouth, a bottle of water appeared in front of her.

This time she didn't even have to look to know it was Conall. He'd been taking very good care of her all night. Making sure she ate, stayed away from any cleverly hidden drugs, and that she was always hydrated. She grabbed the bottle and made room on the stoop so he could sit down beside her. She realized she didn't mind him sitting close. Of course, with Conall she really had no choice. He took up a lot of space on the stoop. At least his shoulders did.

"Feel better now?" she asked as she opened the bottle.

"Yeah. I've recovered from my random act of violence." He looked at her. "Are you okay?"

"Yeah. I'm fine. I almost killed a man, though."

"What?"

She pointed and Conall leaned over her to see. As soon as his body touched hers, she had that same damn reaction. Hard nipples. Wet pussy. It was getting ridiculous.

"What happened?"

She had to force herself to focus. "He kissed me. But it took me by surprise."

She felt the growl before she heard it. Miki dropped her water bottle, accidentally hitting Troy in the back of the head, and grabbed Conall's shoulders before he could leap off the stoop and tear Troy apart.

"Don't you dare! Sara will kill me if you go to prison."

He let her pull him back. His arm brushed her breasts and the gasp was out of her mouth before she could even think about stopping it. His eyes locked with hers. She still had her hands on his shoulders. On a whim, she slid them up his neck, cupping his chin. He was so gorgeous. She felt the strength of him under her hands. The power of the wolf just inside his skin.

He was a piece of ass and he was interested in her.

Maybe she'd been looking at this the wrong way. Maybe she should go to what she knew. Science. How did attraction work? Why could one man force her to knock him on his ass, while another made her want to drop to her knees? Well, there was only one way to find out.

She took a deep breath and pulled him toward her.

Conall stared at her mouth and it didn't seem like he was breathing at all. "Miki..."

"Shhh. I'm testing a theory." And then her mouth was on his. And, yeah, this was definitely different from when Troy kissed her. She'd felt nothing but panic and the slightest trace of revulsion with Troy. But when her tongue connected with Conall's all she wanted was for him to crawl inside her. She leaned back against the stoop, Conall right there with her. Over her. His hands sliding around her back. His arms wrapping around her. She realized he was keeping her back off the hard stone stoop. And every time his tongue stroked hers, she felt it all the way to her clit. She wanted this man. In fact, she had to have him. Preferably now.

She pulled her mouth away from his. She needed to say something sexy and romantic with a mere hint of her vast intelligence. Something that would entice him into bed.

But what came out was, "I wanna fuck."

Conall groaned and buried his face in her neck. "You're killing me, Mik," he finally managed. "Don't do this if you're just messing with my head 'cause you're still pissed or..."

She rubbed her cheek against his silky hair and decided to just go for it. So what if he probably wouldn't want her after all this was over? At least she could say she had a good time. And she knew Conall would be a good time. A *really* good time. She was tired of being respectable and normal. It was boring, and she *did* need to get laid.

So what would Miki the Bartender do here? Easy. She'd be honest. "Do you know what one of the wolves protecting my house back in Texas told me?" she whispered in his ear and she felt his entire body vibrate against hers. "He told me I moaned your name in my sleep. And I realized my hand smelled like I'd been masturbating all night long. No one's ever done that to me before you. No one but you."

Conall slowly untangled himself from her. He didn't look at her. Instead, he pulled away and sat on one of the lower stoops. He dragged his big hands through his hair and she watched him stretch out his big shoulders. Miki sat up and reached her hand out to touch him.

"Don't. Touch. Me."

Miki frowned, a little bit hurt. "Why?"

"Because I'm doing my best to control myself. And if you touch me I'll fuck you right on this stoop, and I don't want to do that to you in front of your friends. So, don't touch me right now."

"I see." She scratched her neck. "But you know, we can go back to the hotel and then you can fuck me anywhere or any way you want."

Yeah. That was clear. The next move was his.

Miki stood up and walked back into the house. She got as far as the coffee pot before she felt herself lifted off her feet and thrown over Conall's shoulder. The entire room cheered as they left. She waved at Amy who drunkenly gave her a thumbs-up.

Conall arrived at the SUV in what seemed like seconds, then he opened the door, dumped her in, and stopped only long enough to say, "Not another word from you. Not one."

She watched as he went around the SUV to get in. She was almost positive he had no idea his fangs were out.

Chapter Thirteen

Surprisingly, he wasn't pulled over. He used to ride sportsbikes that could hit two hundred miles per hour and he was pretty sure he'd never gone as fast on one of them as he did in the SUV. But Miki finally pushed him over the edge. He prayed she didn't back down now. He wasn't sure he could take it. He'd almost dragged her into Craig's bathroom and took her there, but he forced himself to get under some kind of control. Although the wolf was having a full-on fistfight with the man in him.

Tires squealed as he turned into the hotel parking lot and took the first spot he saw. He got out, went around to the passenger side, and dragged Miki out. She didn't say a word as he tossed her over his shoulder and went into the hotel. The hotel staff watched him quietly. He knew they wanted to say something to him about carrying a woman into their four-star hotel as if he were a caveman. But he knew none of them had the guts to say a word. He could only imagine the expression on his face.

But Miki was torturing him. Whether she meant to or not, she was torturing him. And until he was buried deep inside of her there would be no rest for him. No solace. No peace.

He didn't even wait for the elevator. He took the stairs up ten flights and wasn't even out of breath by the time he got to his door. He swiped his keycard, went in and tossed Miki on the bed.

She seemed unfazed by it all as she watched him with those inquisitive brown eyes. He didn't want to make the same mistake he'd almost made that morning. So he went to his bag, dug through the few clothes he had packed, and grabbed the brown paper bag of condoms Sara had shoved in it as he walked out the den door. At the time he thought she was simply being hopeful.

He tossed the bag on the floor by the bed. Miki started to say something but he cut her off.

"Not a word."

She surprisingly fell silent, watching him move to the bed. Her gaze dragged along the length of his body as he dropped to his knees in front of her.

"Lay back."

She shook her head. "I wanna watch you."

He growled and slid his hands under her skirt. He dragged her lace panties off, but left the garters and Docs on. He'd been thinking about going down on her dressed like that since she'd come out of the bathroom. He leaned forward and licked the inside of her thigh just above the stocking. She remained quiet until he pushed her thighs farther apart and his tongue skimmed along the folds of her sex. That's when she gave a low moan and her head fell back. She used one arm to keep herself propped up while the other grabbed the back of his head and pushed him forward.

He pulled back a bit. "Miki." Her eyes focused on him. "You said you wanted to watch me. So watch me."

From the way her breathing changed and the expression on her face, he had a feeling he'd pushed her that much closer to coming. Which was good, because he wasn't sure how much longer he could hold out. He needed to be inside this woman before he lost his mind.

His tongue slid inside her tight pussy. It was wet and hot and tasted so good. Miki's hand tightened in his hair, pulling him close as his hands slid under her to cup her ass. He dragged her to him, his hands gripping her tight. She moaned in response, one leg over his shoulder, the other propped up on the bed.

Limber girl, he thought happily.

He licked her slowly, enjoying the sweet taste of her. The smell. He felt her body begin to shake when her orgasm broke around him. She made low, guttural sounds from the back of her throat as he used his tongue to stretch out her climax as long as he could.

When she tugged on his hair, trying to pull him up, he knew she was ready for him. He leaned back on his haunches, and stared at her. He needed her to make this move. He needed to know this was what she really wanted.

She ran her small hand across his jaw and down his neck. Then, slowly, leaned forward and began to lick her juices off his mouth and chin.

I'll take that as a yes. He slid his hands to her waist and lifted her shirt up, lifting it over her head and tossing it across the room. She pulled away from him, backing up on the bed to yank off her skirt, the stockings, the Docs, all of it. Which was good. He wanted her completely naked. And completely his.

Miki tossed her Docs across the room as Conall yanked his T-shirt over his head, then he tackled his jeans. She'd never been this horny for anybody before in her life. She felt almost...desperate. Which was good because when he dropped his pants and she saw the size of his raging hard-on, she knew she was in for quite the workout.

But something inside her had changed. Here she was kneeling on the bed, completely naked, and she didn't care. For the first time in her life, she really couldn't give a flying fuck about anything or anyone except Conall and his huge dick.

She smiled and crooked her index finger at him. He didn't need any more prompting than that. Whipping on a condom, he was in her arms within seconds. They both fell back on the bed, his hot mouth sucking at her breast. Every time his tongue swiped across her nipple, she felt it all the way down to her clit.

She heard growling, but it wasn't Conall. It was her.

When she growled, he thought he would finally snap. He wanted to wait a bit. Make it all special and romantic, but who the hell was he kidding? He was wolf and she was fucking hot. He rose over her, his arms on either side of her shoulders. Miki's body arched to meet his as he thrust inside of her, embedding himself deep.

She seemed so small under him. Small and beautiful. Miki looked up and gasped in surprise. Her hand reached up and touched his forehead. "Wolf eyes," she whispered. His eyes must have shifted, but she wasn't frightened. She leaned up and, unable to reach his mouth, she kissed his chest and neck. He trembled, holding his body rigid. His cock still buried in her tight pussy. He wanted to stay this way forever.

Her legs wrapped around his waist, her ankles locking at the base of his spine. Her fingers digging into his ass, keeping him deep inside her. When he couldn't wait any longer, he began to stroke in and out. She felt so good, he thought he'd come any second. But he held on for her. Of course, it didn't help when she began moving her hips and moaning his name. Yup. The woman was definitely trying to kill him.

Her tongue swiped across his nipple and he almost unraveled. "Oh God, Miki, baby. Don't." He was holding on by a thread.

She smiled against his flesh before sucking his nipple into her mouth. He felt his canines extend, and he desperately fought his desire to mark her. He didn't want to do that to her. She was full human and he needed to know it was what she wanted. But he knew no other woman had ever made him like this. This crazy. This desperate. He'd worked so long and hard to control his every instinct, and this one clearly unstable woman had completely destroyed all that.

As his claws ripped the sheets underneath them, he knew at that very moment he loved her.

She could hear the sheets ripping under her. His claws were out. His fangs. His eyes had shifted. Who knew this would be such a turn on? And it was. It was like her entire body was on fire for him. And only him.

She liked making him crazy. As crazy as he made her. She bit into the flesh of his chest and he moaned and snarled all at the same time. He pounded into her harder, a delicious punishment for working so hard to make him come.

Her orgasm slammed into her like a runaway train. So hard she ripped flesh off his back with her nails and screamed in release. He came a moment after, his back arching, a howl torn from his throat. Knowing she made him howl...no, you really couldn't get cooler than that.

He dropped on top of her. His whole body clearly too devastated to move. She didn't complain. She didn't realize how much she'd like such a big guy lying on top of her. She felt warm. Cozy. Safe. After a few minutes, he rolled off. His warmth gone, the sweat on her body chilled. She almost told him to roll his ass back.

They were both silent for several moments. Then she chuckled. She couldn't help herself. Then he started to chuckle. Then they both started laughing outright.

"I was right," she finally managed. "Viking."

With a playful growl, he launched himself at her, knocking both of them off the bed.

Chapter Fourteen

"Mmmhm, Conall."

Conall's eyes snapped open. *What in hell?* He turned over slowly and looked at her. He could see her clearly in the pitch-black room. She lay on her side, facing him. And sound asleep.

He raised an eyebrow. The woman was definitely out cold, but he'd heard her voice. Was she dreaming about him? They'd just had several hours of seriously hard-core sex, she should be just sleeping. And she definitely shouldn't be having wet dreams about him still.

She suddenly stretched, turning so her back rested against the bare mattress. The ruined sheets had hit the floor hours ago. While she stretched, her back arched, presenting those adorable breasts of hers to him like an offering from the gods. He leaned down and licked one. Just a slow swipe. Her back arched more and again she moaned his name.

He stared at her, loving his wolf eyes because he could see her without turning on a light and ruining the moment. She was the most beautiful woman he'd ever seen. It wasn't simply her looks either. Hell, those could go and he wouldn't miss them. It was something else. It was her. She was raw and rude and who she was. The wolf in him loved that. Loved her. When she was around, the wolf in him wanted to lie down and put his head in her lap. And he didn't have to hide who he was. She seemed to relish the rawness he'd always worked so hard to keep bottled up.

"Conall?" It sounded almost like she was pleading with him. Christ, what exactly was his dream self up to? He noticed her arms were still over her head, like someone held them in place. He growled and she smiled in her sleep, her lust reaching out and grabbing him around the cock.

He reached over and ran his finger gently across her nipple. It hardened further under his touch but she didn't wake. He pinched the nipple between his thumb and forefinger. She wiggled a bit, but she slept on.

Yeah, he liked the way she slept.

He brought his mouth down to her breast, grasping her nipple gently between his teeth. He let his tongue flick over it again and again and then he sucked. She made desperate sounds from the back of her throat, but miraculously she was still out cold.

He ran his hand down her stomach and in between her thighs. She moaned as his forefinger circled her clit then flicked it. She almost came off the bed, so he grasped her arms and held them down.

He briefly closed his eyes. He never thought he'd meet someone like Miki. Someone strong enough to be his woman. His mate. But she was. She was everything he'd ever hoped for. And it didn't hurt she was one wicked fuck.

He worked her clit with his fingers and her breasts with his mouth and tongue. But whatever was happening in her dream had already brought her halfway to climax. All he was doing was providing the last little push she needed.

She shuddered. Actually, her entire body did. Then her legs began to shake. She was coming, and he pulled back enough so he could watch her. She always came hard and loud, and looked beautiful doing it.

He stayed with her until her body settled down. Then she smiled in her sleep and sighed...his name.

If he physically could have, he would have come himself. That's what the woman did to him. Instead, he decided right then and there. He was going to marry Miki Kendrick. He just had to convince her. And, hell, how hard could that be?

Miki felt warm lips against hers. She sighed and opened her eyes, giving them a few seconds to adjust to the darkness. His lips moved gently down her neck and she felt that wonderful hair of his rubbing across her flesh. God, she loved the feel of his hair against her body. She wanted to run her hands through it, but she couldn't since her arms were pinned above her head.

"Um...Conall?"

"Um...Miki?"

"What's the deal with my arms?"

"It was the only way to keep you pinned to the bed?"

"See, statements like that really freak me out."

"You started it."

"I started what?"

"A woman moans your name in her sleep, it's really hard to ignore her."

Now this was getting embarrassing. "God, did I jack off in my sleep again?" This wasn't a mental disorder was it? Like being a sociopath or a schizophrenic.

"No. But I thought you could use a little assistance with that."

"Oh." She thought she had dreamed all that. She was glad

she hadn't because it fuckin' rocked.

He kissed her mouth again, released her arms then sat up, his back against the headboard. He reached over to the side table and grabbed something. She heard a tearing sound and realized he'd grabbed a condom.

"What are you doing, Viking?"

"Get up here, Kendrick."

"I'm sleeping."

"Not anymore you're not. Let's go. Haul it out."

"Well, you are quite the romantic." She pulled herself up and crawled into his lap.

"You want romantic? How about 'I wanna fuck.'"

"Asshole," she muttered as she straddled his waist and lowered herself onto him. Her pussy already wet, his big cock slid in easily. She let go a rough moan. Christ, he felt so good inside her.

"You okay?" His voice was rough like hers now. She couldn't see him very well in the dark, but she could see his eyes. She could feel him.

"Are you kidding?"

He licked her neck and grabbed her around the waist. "I wanted to fuck and kiss you all at the same time without arching my back, and I was thinking this might be the best way to do it."

He didn't seem bothered by their height differences. In fact, it seemed as if he enjoyed the challenge.

"Kiss me, Mik."

She leaned forward, her arms around his neck, her breasts against his chest. She slowly ran her tongue along his bottom lip, then slid to the top. He tried to capture her mouth with his, but she pulled back, drawing one of his growls. She really enjoyed teasing him. He leaned back and waited. She touched his lips again with her tongue. He tasted so good. But when he tried to kiss her, she moved away.

"What the hell are you doing?"

"Having a little fun."

He groaned. One of frustration, his head rubbing against her cheek then her neck. "Dammit, woman. Kiss me."

"All right," she laughed. "Don't whine."

She kissed him and his hands tightened on her waist, his cock expanding even more inside her. She dug her hands into his hair and pulled him closer. It was like they were both trying to slide into each other's skin.

He held her tight, his tongue stroking hers. She felt how much he wanted her. Needed her, even. No one had ever reacted this way to her before. Or made her feel the same.

She slowly began to ride him, her hips moving against him, her pussy tightening around his cock. He moaned and his fingers dug deep into her flesh. It hurt, but in a good way. A damn good way.

She didn't rush it and he didn't ask her to. It seemed like they were both just enjoying the moment. Enjoying each other.

"Miki-baby?"

She liked when he called her that. She realized it was his nickname for her. And she liked that she had a nickname. "Mhhmm?"

"You don't have any school plans tomorrow, do you?"

"No. Why?"

"Just wondering what would happen if we kept this going for the next four or five hours."

Miki chuckled. "I don't sleep, Viking. Not really. So it wouldn't matter to me."

He licked her neck. Nipped her earlobe. And she kept riding him. "You just need somebody to wear you out."

She snorted. "Yeah. Good luck with that."

They both froze. *Dammit.*

"Uh, Conall..."

"Too late! The gauntlet's been laid. I accept your challenge."

"No. No. Now let's be rational about this." She tried to squirm away from him, but his grip tightened like a delicious vice. He wasn't letting her go anywhere and she loved every minute of it.

"Dogs aren't rational, baby. We're dogs. We just want a job." He squeezed her ass and she squeaked. "And I just found mine..."

Chapter Fifteen

Her damn cell phone ringing woke him up. He wondered where she was and why she hadn't answered it yet. Then he realized she was asleep on his back. Not against his back. *On* his back. Out cold. It took some work, but he'd finally worn her out enough to get some more sleep. He had to admit, though, it was quite the party getting her there.

He gazed at the clock. They'd been asleep for about six hours. Not a big deal for him, but he knew she only got about three or four hours of sleep a night, if she were lucky.

He loved having her on his back, her soft breasts pressing against his flesh. Her arms thrown loosely over his shoulders. Her legs stretched out on top of his, although her toes barely passed the back of his knees.

The phone stopped ringing. But now it kept making a beeping sound that made it clear there was a message waiting. That would get on his nerves real quick. He hated to wake her, but she should get her phone and he really had to pee.

"Miki-baby." She stirred a little. Her head turned and her lips pressed against his naked back. Immediately he got hard again. How? His cock should have fallen off with the workout it got last night. "Mik."

"Mmmhmm?" She sounded sated.

"Your phone's beeping."

"What?" He felt the top half of her body lift off his back and his skin barked at the loss of her. "Oh."

She slid off his back, her groin briefly dragging across his ass. He was pretty sure nothing would ever feel better than that.

She flipped the phone open and quickly checked her messages. She frowned and speed-dialed a number.

"Hey, Craig. It's me. Whasup?"

Conall sat up, watching her move as she held the phone. He liked watching her move.

"Yeah. I can meet you. But not now. How about breakfast at the diner across from the Watson Suites? Yeah. Yeah. That works. Cool. See ya." She closed her cell phone.

"Everything okay?"

She shrugged. A casual move. All the tension she had when he'd touched her at the club seemed to have drifted away. "Not sure. Craig is weird. It could be something serious or something he thinks is serious that isn't. It's always a crapshoot with him."

She yawned and stretched. He watched her body go taut and heard the little high-pitched noise she made at the back of her throat. Before he knew it, he'd slipped out of bed and was heading for her. But she saw him coming and stepped away.

"I don't think so."

He almost groaned. She wasn't going back into "stay away from Conall" mode again, was she?

"Oh, yeah?"

"Yeah." She walked to the bathroom. "You've got something else to do."

"Which is?"

She looked at him from the bathroom doorway. "Help with

the soap."

∞

One shower and three orgasms later, they'd made it to the diner. Conall kept staring at her over his orange juice while they waited for their food. She tried to ignore him but the man didn't make it easy. Especially when he kept growling.

"Stop doing that."

"Stop doing what?"

"Growling."

"It makes you wet, doesn't it?"

She tried to glare at him over her cup of coffee but one look at that beautiful, wicked face and it took all her strength not to nail him right there in the booth.

"Bastard."

"Not according to my mother."

Conall was deep into his third helping of waffles and bacon—the man could really pack it away—when her friends showed up. They all tried to squeeze into the booth, but with Conall on one side that was just not happening. So Ben and Craig pulled chairs to the side and Miki made Kenny and Amy sit next to her. There was no way she'd let Amy anywhere near Conall.

"So?"

Her friends exchanged glances and immediately she began to worry.

"What?"

"I'll tell her." Amy looked at her. "Now don't freak out, but we found a password-protected folder in Leucrotta's computer.

It had your information in it."

"What do you mean? What information?"

"Everything. Social Security number, bank accounts, gym membership."

Kenny Liu leaned forward. "Plus a detailed list of your daily activities the last five or six months. And by the way, you live a really boring life."

"We did a trace and it seems like he hired a PI. Someone local to you," Ben added.

Conall pushed his nearly empty plate away and leaned back in the booth. He wasn't saying anything, just calmly listening to her friends.

"We also found a folder for Angelina," Craig muttered softly. "It had the same kind of info."

She should have been freaking out. She should have been screaming her head off and seeing all possible disastrous scenarios that could occur. And although part of her brain was working on contingency plans should things get out of hand, she didn't feel the need to start any kind of global panic. She knew Conall and the Pack would do what they could to protect her and Angelina. She also knew she was too mean to take crap from anybody. She liked the fact that she was finally starting to enjoy that part of herself. It's what made her who she was.

Miki nodded. "Okay. Thanks."

"That's it? 'Okay. Thanks.' That's all we're getting?" Amy looked at her. "You're not freaking out, which tells me you're not surprised."

"I'm not surprised. But that's all I can really tell you."

"Bullshit."

"I'm not going to argue about this with you, Amy. So let it fuckin' go."

"What else do you need us to do?" Kenny Liu cut in before Amy could start ranting.

For the first time since her friends arrived, Conall spoke. "Nothing. Don't do anything. And clean up your tracks. They should never know you were there."

"They? Who's they?" As the King of Paranoia, Craig was all over that little statement. But Miki knew she couldn't tell him the truth. It wasn't her truth to tell. So she lied.

"Mafia."

Conall's head snapped around and stared at her. She gave the smallest eyebrow raise.

"Mafia?" Amy turned her body in the booth so she could stare Miki in the face. "*The* Mafia? You expect us to buy that the Mafia is out to get you?"

Conall leaned forward, his most innocent expression on that dangerously misleading face. "Hey. That's not something we'd lie about."

Miki looked at Amy. She had to. If she stared at Conall a second longer, she would start giggling hysterically.

He returned his gaze to Craig. "And if they find out you were there, we'll find your body in the back of a Cadillac with your tongue cut out."

Miki bit the inside of her cheek and kicked Conall under the table.

She watched the range of emotions pass over her friends' faces. Ben had stopped listening, which meant he was bored. Kenny Liu appeared truly concerned. Craig looked like he would pass out from the panic. And Amy restlessly tapped her fingers against the Formica table and glowered.

"You must be insane if you expect us to buy that load of shit."

"There's a lot about me you guys don't know."

"You're lying, Kendrick. You *and* Conan the Barbarian."

Miki and Conall looked innocently at each other then back at her friends.

She shook her head sadly. "It hurts me that you think I'm lying."

Conall sighed. "It hurts us both."

She would have really lost it then if she and Conall weren't busy kicking each other under the table.

℘

"The Mafia? Was that the best you could do?" They'd started laughing as soon as Amy and the rest of them left. Ten minutes later and they were still laughing.

"Dude, I was desperate. I needed something and Amy wasn't backing off. I know her."

"Fine. Whatever." Conall grabbed her hand. "Let's go back to the hotel and fuck some more."

"Actually, I have another idea."

Why didn't he like the sound of that? "A *better* idea?"

"Probably not." She held up a small slip of paper. "But an idea just the same."

"What's that?"

"Leucrotta's address. Let's do a drive-by."

"Shooting?" He wouldn't put it past her.

"No, you nut case. Let's go check him out."

"No way, baby. Something happens to you, Zach will have my ass because Sara will have his." He looked down into that adorable face of hers. "And I might miss you a little myself."

"Gee. Thanks." Miki smirked at him. "Look. We can do this one of two ways. We can go there now. Together. Check it out for our amusement. Or you can find yourself passed out in a pool of your own vomit in the bathroom while I risk life and limb going there by myself."

Conall stared down at her. "You'd drug me again?"

"Sure. I'd only have to wrap it in bacon."

Conall wanted to be insulted, but she was just so damn cute. "I can't afford to have you traipsing that tight ass of yours around a Clan den."

"And I have no desire to get too close. I have no guns. No knives. No hand grenades. I'm defenseless. But we need to check out the enemy. We need to find out who these people are. I don't believe in spending my life hiding or running."

He believed that. He saw why Sara and Miki were friends. Miki was as tough as any wolf he knew, she simply found a different way to survive. But still, he didn't want her to get hurt. "I don't know, Mik."

She smiled at him and he felt his cock rear its ugly head. "Please, Conall...baby. For me."

He laughed again. "You're fuckin' shameless."

She took the car keys out of his jeans pocket. "Come on, baby." She jangled the keys at him. "Come on. Let's go for a ride!"

"I swear to God, woman. You make one crack about hanging my head out the window..."

She frowned and he could tell she'd been all set to do just that. "Damn."

She wondered how long they would play twenty questions

as she led him to Leucrotta's house. She'd memorized every street map of Seattle and the surrounding areas. Didn't take much. She only had to examine a map once to know every detail.

"Where did you learn to shoot?" Again with more questions. Why was he so interested? They'd already gone through these types of questions just the other night, but then he was still trying to get into her pants. Now that he was in, she wasn't quite sure why he was still so curious.

Are booty calls supposed to be this chatty?

"The Marines."

"You were in the Marines?" He didn't have to sound so shocked.

"No."

"Did you date a Marine?"

"No."

He seemed relieved by that answer, which confused her even more.

"Was your father a Marine?"

"I don't know. I didn't know the man."

"Really?"

"He tried to contact me once after high school. But I told him to go to hell. I had no desire to meet a man who at twenty-six dated a sixteen-year-old girl, got her pregnant and then dumped her."

It had been a good thing she didn't meet her father then. Nineteen years old, in college, with full access to the biotech labs. Between that and her association with Craig and the guys, she would have hurt the man. As it was she remembered a late night of hiding one of her creations in what was now Craig's personal lab. Had to. The military wanted to get their hands on it. Of course, Sara and Angelina still thought she was delusional when she said Black Ops would be coming for her one day. Little did they know.

"I can understand that. Did your mother love him?"

"Tragically, yes."

He fell silent on that point and apparently decided to let it go. "Angelina dated a Marine?"

Miki rolled her eyes. "Nope. They're on the List."

"What List?"

"You know, it's right in your face. You just refuse to see."

Conall stopped at a red light and looked at her. Then he grinned. A big, beautiful grin. "Your mother was a Marine."

"And finally my Cro-Magnon man enters the twenty-first century where women are in the military."

"*Your* Cro-Magnon man?"

She stared out the window so she didn't have to see his Viking grin. She wasn't going to start liking him. Not really liking him. A passing "I don't hate you enough to kill you" association was fine and dandy. But liking him like she liked Sara or Amy or Angelina or even Craig was out of the question.

The light changed and he moved forward. "Okay. So I missed it. The obvious. So she taught you to hunt?"

"No. I learned to hunt from my grandmother. Her father was a tracker and moonshiner. My mother taught me how to shoot. Every Marine's a rifleman, ya know." She shrugged. "By the time I was twelve, I'd skin my own kills."

"That's lovely."

Miki nodded, ignoring his sarcasm. "I'd cut off the pelts. Strip the flesh. Freeze it. We'd have deer meat for weeks." She looked at him. "And sometimes I'd make little hats from their heads."

Conall pulled over on a quiet suburban street. "Okay. This conversation's ending now." He shuddered. "Freaky woman." He glanced around. "We're getting near. I can smell them."

"We're not going to get any closer?"

"No way." He shut off the car and handed her the keys. "If I'm not back in twenty minutes, leave and don't go back to the hotel. Understand me?"

"Yes, my liege."

He glared at her. "Smart ass."

"What are you going to do?"

He shrugged. "Stay downwind."

Then he was out of the car and disappearing down the street. Miki put her feet up on the dashboard and waited.

∞

Conall dumped his clothes behind an empty house with a For Sale sign in the front, shifted, and trotted the rest of the way to Leucrotta's house. He knew as soon as he hit their street. The smell almost overpowered him. It took him a bit to discover the disgusting scent came from the pasty white secretions on almost every tree and home he passed. *When these guys mark their territory, they really mark their territory.* He soon realized almost every house on the street belonged to this Clan.

The street was pretty deserted and Conall assumed the majority of members were at their day jobs. He slipped into a backyard and tracked his way to one of the houses where he actually heard activity. There was a high fence, but he found a tear in the wood he could look through. A good-sized property with a pool, it seemed like any other normal high-priced suburban home. Yet he was witness to one of the most disturbing things he'd ever seen.

Four females—*they were females right?*—were in a full-on fistfight. Blood was drawn and he could hear bones breaking. The other females, about fourteen of them, watched impassively. Even more freakish was the vicious brawl going on between the children. Not just a shoving match or putting little Johnny's head in the toilet, but teeth and claws used to cause permanent harm.

He thought about growing up as wolf pup. He remembered wrestling with Zach. One time, when they were no more than six, Zach accidentally knocked him down a flight of stairs and the poor kid cried for hours until Conall could walk again and remember his first name.

But what Conall watched now was a brutal display of pure, unadulterated aggression. These were definitely not people to fuck with lightly.

Then the wind shifted. The fighting stopped. The aggression stopped. And all attention focused on him at the fence.

He took several steps back, spun around, and took off.

It was time to call on his Pack.

ⅎ

Miki got tired of waiting in the SUV, so she sat on the stoop instead. She couldn't stop thinking about the previous night. So that's what Sara and Angie meant about getting your world rocked. No wonder people were obsessed with sex. Now she was obsessed with sex. Sex with Conall.

She felt Conall as wolf come up next to her. She didn't even bother glancing at him as he settled down next to her. He nuzzled her arm.

"What are you doing?"

He licked her chin. "Are you going to tell me what happened or not?"

Conall lay down next to her and rolled on his back. She sighed. This was so demeaning.

Still refusing to look at him, she rubbed his belly. Conall clearly loved it. She could feel his whole body wiggling under her fingers as they played across his stomach and chest.

"This is ridiculous. Just shift and tell me what you saw." She finally turned to look at him. His tongue was hanging out, the happiest grin on his face. And it suddenly occurred to her that this dog was not a wolf. And it definitely wasn't Conall. "Oh for shit's sake—"

"What are you doing?"

Miki cringed. She looked up and kept looking up until she could see Conall's face. As human, he stood on the other side of her. Wet, like he'd been swimming. Fully dressed. And fully disgusted.

"Uh...playing with this cute doggie?"

"You thought he was me, didn't you!"

"Don't get testy. It could have been you."

"It's a golden retriever," he growled. "I can't talk to you right now." He stormed back to the SUV.

Miki looked at the golden laying comfortably next to her. "Thanks a lot."

"Are we going?"

Miki stood up as the dog bolted at Conall's yelled question, his tail between his legs. She couldn't even spare him a glance. She walked back to the SUV and over to Conall. Normally she wouldn't care if she hurt someone's feelings, except maybe Sara and Angelina's but they had hides made of stone. But for some reason, having Conall mad at her gave her a lousy feeling.

She stood in front of him. "I'm sorry."

"I'm not a dog."

"I know that. I just wasn't paying attention. I didn't even look at him."

"You know, we don't all look alike." She didn't bother to point out that they were all part of the *canis lupus* family. That would probably just piss him off more.

"I know." On a whim, she wrapped her arms around his waist and laid her head against his chest. She felt his body grudgingly begin to relax as his arms wrapped around her. She had never been an affectionate person, but for some reason she found it easy and kind of nice with Conall. "I'm really, *really* sorry. Really."

He chuckled. "Not sure you said enough reallys."

She felt the dampness of his T-shirt. "Why are you wet?"

"Wind shifted. I had to use someone's pool to get them off my scent."

"Smart. So what did you find out? Was Conridge right?"

"They're more than barbaric. They're scary. Scarier than I remember. Maybe you could do some research on that computer of yours. See what else you can find out."

But she already had some knowledge, so why wait? Miki closed her eyes. She could visualize one of her favorite books. *Encyclopedia of Mammals.* She saw the pages turn as if she had the book in her lap. She flipped to the section on hyenas and read what was there.

"They're matriarchal. Extremely aggressive, which we already know. They don't get along like wolves or Pride, though. There is a lot of in-fighting. Well, this explains a lot. The male-female sex organs look very similar. At one time it was believed they were hermaphrodites, but they're not. Oooh."

"What?"

"The cubs are born with a full set of teeth and they start fighting from the time they are pushed out of the womb. Sometimes two will fight while the mother is cleaning off a third. How freaking interesting is that?"

Conall frowned. He should be mad. She'd mistaken a golden retriever for him. Not even a German shepherd or a husky, but a golden. But he was too busy loving the feel of her arms wrapped around his waist and the sudden realization she just pulled hyena knowledge out of her pretty tight ass.

"How exactly did you know all that?"

"I have a good memory."

"It sounded like you were reading from a book. You were, weren't you?" He could feel her get uneasy. "You just read a book in your head, didn't you?"

"I'm not sure what you—"

"Exactly how high is your IQ anyway?"

Miki cleared her throat. "One hundred and seventy-eight."

Last he heard one hundred and forty was hitting genius level. *Damn.*

"Why didn't you go to some special school or something?"

"My grandmother didn't believe in them. But I always took advanced classes and some college courses." Her body was tense against his. She was waiting for some kind of weird repercussion to her admission. She didn't seem to realize he really could give a shit. As far as he was concerned this only meant their kids would be smart shapeshifters.

"Well, so you don't get too cocky, I myself often complete

the *TV Guide* crossword puzzle." He puffed out his chest. "In pen."

Miki burst out laughing. He loved making her laugh. Her entire body became involved. Kind of like when she had an orgasm.

Conall kissed her forehead. "Let's get out of here before they—oh, shit."

"What?" She pulled out of his arms and turned to see what he was looking at. Not a pretty sight. The hyenas had done something he'd never seen before and he hoped to never see again.

They'd sent their children to hunt them.

Six of them stood in the middle of the street in front of her and Conall. A quick look behind them and Miki saw three more.

It was broad daylight in a nice, quiet suburban neighborhood. Yet she felt trapped in a desert in the dead of night.

Miki didn't mince words. "Let's get in the car and run the fuckers down."

Conall gaped at her. "They're kids. I can't hit kids. And I'm really hoping you can't either."

Miki sighed. No. She couldn't mow down a bunch of kids. But she wished she could. Because they may be children, but they were the scariest fucking things she'd ever seen. She always wondered what kind of kids were homeschooled. These guys must make up a huge percentage. She had a feeling the fangs they were showing couldn't retract until they were much older.

"Fine. You want to be Mr. Nice Guy and not hit the kids, then that leaves only one option."

"Which is?"

She quickly snatched the door open to the SUV, dived inside to dig into her backpack, and pulled out her house keys.

"Now I don't want you to take this personally," she ordered as she scrambled back out.

Conall didn't look at her, too busy watching the slowly advancing cubs. "Take what personally?"

Miki pulled off the small plastic controller attached to her keys. She showed it to him.

"Stop the Bark?" He smirked even as his canine teeth extended and his eyes shifted to wolf. "You're kidding, right? That may work with that golden you were loving up, but I doubt it will do much to the rest of us."

Miki cleared her throat. "I amped it up a bit in case those full-blooded wolves got a little cranky Sara wasn't around anymore." She pushed the button and hoped Conall could forgive her.

He went down first. His hands over his ears, his fangs bared, a howl torn from his throat. Then the hyenas went down screaming. Even the adult females watching from the sidelines hit the ground, their androgynous bodies writhing in pain. To Miki it was silent. She couldn't hear anything and she felt nothing.

Well, at least now she knew it worked.

Miki grabbed Conall by the neck of his T-shirt and tugged, hoping he could manage to get up since she'd never be able to lift him by herself. He dragged himself up and crawled into the SUV. She followed, her finger still on the button. She adjusted the seat so her feet reached the gas pedal, and then she started the SUV. She finally released the button as she drove off, making sure to avoid the cubs lying in the street.

Once they were safely away, she dropped her keys and the device back in her bag.

Conall looked at her. His fangs still out, his eyes red rimmed. "You call that 'amping it up a bit'?"

She shrugged. "Be thankful. It could have been worse. I've been thinking about mating it with a stun gun. You know, for shits and giggles."

He leaned back in the seat. "You're a dangerous woman, Miki Kendrick."

She smiled. She got the feeling he meant that as a compliment.

Chapter Sixteen

Conall had been watching her for the last ten minutes. She'd asked for grape but he could only find cherry. A cherry ice pop. He'd handed it to her after getting back with their lunch from the deli next door.

Once they got safely back to the hotel, and his ears stopped ringing, he'd talked to Sara. Filled her in on the information discovered by Miki's hacker friends. Told her about what he saw at the Clan den. She was unfazed by the fact Miki had gone with him on his little excursion. Seemed she trusted her friend as much as he did. And he did trust Miki. That realization kept playing through his brain. Sara told him she would talk to Zach once he got back from hunting, and they'd get some Pack members up to Seattle as soon as possible. Then she gave him a direct command. Something she never did. Protect Miki. She didn't care what he had to do or who he had to kill. She wanted Miki safe.

As far as Conall was concerned, not a problem.

So, he'd settled in to eat the first of the three giant sandwiches with chips and beer he'd bought. But he hadn't taken a bite. Not once he noticed her and that freakin' ice pop.

Stomach down on the bed, she worked on her laptop doing more research on hyenas. She had both hands on the keyboard, forcing her to suck on the phallic-shaped ice pop only using her mouth. In and out. In and out. And the slurping sounds—she had to be kidding! He'd bet money Miki had no clue what she was doing to him.

Eventually, he couldn't take it anymore.

"I want you to do that to me."

She didn't look up from her laptop. "Do what," she mumbled around the pop.

"Suck my cock like you're sucking that ice pop."

She froze, her hands pausing over the keyboard. Slowly her eyes lifted, focusing on him. She stared at him for several moments. Then she pulled the ice pop out of her mouth, making sure to include a wet "pop" sound when she did.

"That's quite the request."

"It's not a request."

Miki grinned, her teeth catching her bottom lip. "I see. A demand." She pushed the pop past her lips, long and slow, and pulled it out just as slowly. "Interesting."

Miki slipped off the bed and walked toward him. Suddenly his cell phone went off. They both looked at it. Then they dived for it. But Miki was smaller and faster. She grabbed it and flipped it open.

"Hello? Hi, Zach."

Conall shook his head and waved her off, his big body dropping heavily into a nearby chair. His now-painful hard-on nearly ripping through his jeans. "Bathroom! I'm in the bathroom!" he mouthed desperately.

"No. No. He's around. Let me grab him for you."

He'd kill her.

Miki put the phone behind her, using her ass to cover the mouthpiece. She leaned in close to Conall, whispering right against his ear.

"You're going to talk to him. And you're going to be like you always are. And if you can't hold on a conversation. Or if you let him know I'm going down on you...I stop."

He wanted to come from that alone, especially when her tongue reached out and swiped across his ear.

She handed him the phone and slipped the ice pop back in her mouth. He held the phone by his ear but hadn't spoken yet as he watched her kneel in front of him. She undid his jeans and he raised his hips so she could get them off. So busy staring at her, wondering what she was going to do next, he completely forgot about Zach until she motioned to the phone with her head.

"Hey, Zach."

"Hey. I just talked to Sara. You guys okay?"

Conall nodded his answer.

Miki pulled the pop out of her mouth. "I don't think he can see your nodding," she whispered.

He tried to focus. "Yeah. We're fine."

Miki ran the ice pop down the underside of his cock and he thought he would jump out of his skin. *Evil bitch.*

"Good. All right. We've pulled about eight of our guys to send your way. That should be enough until you guys get back. Sara was ready to head up there herself, but there's no fuckin' way I'm letting her ass out of my sight."

"That sounds...fine."

She swiped the pop across the tip and then her tongue swiped right after it.

"I just wish I could figure out what the hell they're doing. Lions are their enemies, we should be allies. I'll talk to the older wolves. See if they can help us out here. And you make sure you watch your back."

He pushed his bare feet into the carpeted floor. "You got it."

Zach paused. Then, "You sound distracted. Is she wearing on you?"

Conall gritted his teeth as Miki's tongue followed wherever she put the ice pop. "You have no idea."

"I warned you about her. You can do better anyway. She doesn't deserve you." Good old supportive Zach with the worst timing *ever*.

"Is she at least talking to you now?"

Conall's head fell back as Miki sucked the tip into her mouth, her teeth lightly grazing over the ridges, her tongue swirling over it.

"Sometimes," he managed.

"Well, don't worry about it. I'll hook you up with a sure thing when you get back."

"Sure," he barely bit back a groan as she took all of him into her mouth—and hummed. "Sounds great."

Zach began to ramble about...something. Who the fuck knew? Conall gave some non-committal noises. Thankfully, Miki let him get away with it, probably because he kept his voice relatively steady. But he had no idea how much longer he would be able to keep that up. Especially once she tossed the ice pop, wrapped that soft hand of hers around his balls, and lightly squeezed.

"Well, since I've got you why don't we go over the stuff for the new club in Barcelona?"

There was no way he'd be able to stay focused during that conversation. No way in hell. As it was, he was surprised he was still conscious.

"I don't have the stuff with me. Can it wait?" Could Zach hear his panting? He wouldn't be able to hold out much longer.

She was working him and knew it, too. She smiled around his cock when she wasn't sucking him into oblivion.

"Yeah. Sure. Sara just came in anyway. Hold on." There was a muffled sound from the other end of the phone. "Uh...Conall. She has a sudden interest in my pants, so I need to go."

Abruptly, Zach hung up. *Thank God for Sara.* Unlike Zach, *her* timing was impeccable.

Conall threw the phone across the room, dug his hands into Miki's hair, and finally let out his harsh groans. So close, he growled in climax thirty seconds later.

She sucked him clean and then looked up with a smile. "Not bad. The conversation I mean."

Okay. He owed the little brat. Big. Besides that talented mouth of hers had only made him hotter. Just looking at her made him hard all over again.

Conall reached down and picked her up. He kicked his jeans out of the way and carried her to the dresser, placing them both in front of its mirror. He turned her so she faced away from him, pushing her down across the wood.

She smirked at him in the mirror. "Dude. Nice idea, but not quite sure how this is going to work."

The dresser had been built for humans of normal height. Conall wasn't that human and his height was anything but normal. Miki wiggled that tight ass at him, thinking he was stuck.

"Again. The lack of creativity," he teased.

He walked to the closet, grabbed her black leather pumps, the ones with the five-inch heels. He placed them next to her. "Put 'em on."

He caught her fighting that smile again. "I plan to wear

those on Friday."

He leaned into her, his arms on either side, blocking her in. "Do as I tell you and put 'em on."

Miki cleared her throat and stepped into the shoes. She looked at him in the mirror. "Well? Now what?"

He yanked her skirt up and ripped her panties off.

Miki gasped as she held onto the dresser. Conall grabbed a condom from a pile next to his keys and change, and slipped it on. Then he grabbed Miki by her hips and slammed into her from behind.

"God, yes!" she bit out. She had her eyes closed, but Conall wanted her to see everything.

He had one hand on her hip to hold her steady while he wrapped the other in her hair and pulled. "Open your eyes, Miki."

She looked into the mirror and their eyes locked in the reflection. "Watch me." His voice low and rough, he barely recognized it. "Watch me fuck you."

She didn't think it possible, but the man had just made her wetter. But that's what Conall did to her. He made her wetter, hotter. With him she was daring, brave, and kind of slutty. But in a good way.

He made her feel beautiful, hot. When she'd worn the pumps before she always felt stupid. Like a kid wearing her mom's clothes. For the first time, she felt like she *owned* these shoes.

She watched his face as he began to fuck her. It was like there was nowhere else he'd rather be. No one else he'd rather be in. That alone was an aphrodisiac.

She picked up his rhythm quickly, like she always seemed

to with him, and brought her body back as he surged forward. It boggled her mind that she made him crazy like this. "Dead below the waist" Kendrick made someone like Conall, who could have his pick of well-trained bar sluts, out of control.

"Touch yourself, Mik."

She moaned as she watched him in the mirror.

"Do it."

And what exactly was his deal with ordering her around when they were fucking? And what was her deal with not minding? And she didn't mind. Dammit, she was a feminist! Marched on Washington to protect a woman's right to choose, etc., etc. But damn if she didn't love to hear him growl out orders. Although it was never orders for orders' sake. He always made sure she got off. Always made sure he left her satisfied and smiling. The man was a fucking demon in bed.

"Now," he ordered.

She reached her hand between her legs and trembled as her fingers found her clit. She began to massage the sensitive, straining nub. Her panting became louder, harsher. It didn't help that Conall still had a good grip on her hair and every once in awhile, he'd tug.

Sometimes she felt like the sensations were too much. His big cock inside of her, his hands on her, his mouth. Sometimes she thought she couldn't handle one more second of it. Of him. She never wanted to feel this way about anybody. She never wanted her body to be so responsive to just one person. But Conall the Viking had come into her life and blown it completely apart. Now she had no idea what the hell she was going to do.

Conall's hand tightened on her waist and her muscles began to tighten around him.

"Conall." She always said his name when he was inside of her. Always.

"Come for me, Miki-baby." He coaxed her with that rough voice of his. "Come for me."

And she did. Another one of her screaming orgasms only Conall seemed to have the ability to force out of her. She rode that feeling, Conall following right behind her.

They collapsed on top of the dresser, their harsh breathing filling the room.

"So," Miki reached back and patted that amazing ass of his. "How's Zach doing?"

Conall gently wrapped his big arms around her and hugged her close. "Evil bitch."

Chapter Seventeen

Miki opened her eyes and for a minute wondered where she was. Hotel rooms, with their big heavy curtains, were always a little too dark for her. But then she felt Conall's big arm wrapped around her, pulling her close into his even bigger chest.

She relaxed and glanced at the clock. Seven a.m. She'd actually slept six hours. Two days in a row she'd slept longer than three or four hours. Of course, Conall kept wearing her out. *Really* wearing her out.

Was it supposed to be like this? He should've gotten bored by now. Started ignoring her. Plotted a way out that wouldn't involve getting his ass kicked by Sara. She thought they'd started down that road the day before. He'd been watching television while she worked on her computer. He'd been quiet for almost an hour and she found herself debating whether he was ignoring her or giving her space to study. On a whim, she muttered something about not finishing what they'd started against the wall in the first hotel room he had. Before she knew it, he had her pinned against the wall like a butterfly in a display. After that it continued for hours. Against the wall. Against the desk. Face down on the bed. Pushed over the bathroom sink. Bent over a chair. She was pretty sure there wasn't a stick of furniture in the room her ass hadn't been on.

She was so confused. He was confusing her and she didn't know what the hell she was doing. This was not her terrain. Sara and Angelina handled the social stuff and Miki made sure they passed calculus class and didn't get kidnapped by bikers.

But now it was getting harder and harder to separate her body from her heart. Even though she continued to promise herself she wouldn't go down that road. But she made the mistake of listening to those two crazy bitches. What the hell had she been thinking? She knew better. Did she learn nothing from the ninth grade lip-gloss and bloodletting incident?

Yet, she wouldn't trade the last few days she'd spent with Conall for anything in the world. He'd taught her sex was fun, pleasurable and freakin' amazing.

Just thinking about him inside of her made her want to turn over and grab that big cock of his. But then she remembered what she had to do in just a few hours. Get up in front of a bunch of uptight professors who barely tolerated her, wearing a suit she hated, defending a thesis she wasn't sure she believed anymore. And how the hell could she defend something she didn't believe in? Unlike Craig's work, her thesis relied on theory as opposed to hard facts from her own lab work. Who the hell would approve that?

Choking panic began to weigh her down, but she shook it off. She had to get her shit together. She had lists to write. She slipped out from under Conall's arm, found her notes, and sat down to obsess over her future for the next eight-and-a-half hours.

She thought she was being quiet, but thirty minutes into her obsessing Conall woke up. He looked at her with that one eye thing he did first thing in the morning and sighed.

"You're obsessing, aren't you?" Because he'd just woken up, his grumbling voice was even more so. The sound made her wet in seconds. She shook her head and went back to her notebook. She didn't have time for this.

"It's what I'm good at."

Conall stood up, gloriously naked, and walked into the bathroom. He closed the door behind him and, within seconds, Miki heard water running. It was her turn to sigh. *Let the ignoring begin!*

She went back to her notes and was halfway down the page when Conall walked back out of the bathroom and straight over to her. He reached down, took the notebook out of her hand and pulled the T-shirt she had on over her head. He tossed it aside, then picked her up and took her with him into the bathroom.

"What the hell are you doing?"

He closed the door with his foot, and took her to the huge marble tub. The room was steamy from the hot water, the tub filled with bubbles. He sunk them both in and relaxed back. Christ, he hadn't stormed out of the room to get away from her. He'd gone off to make her a bubble bath.

"Conall?"

"Miki?"

"I should be preparing. Or panicking. Or both. Probably both."

"Forget panic. It's a waste of energy. And prepare what exactly? You've got a freakin' photographic memory, Mik. You're telling me you don't already know each and every detail from your thesis, your textbooks, and your notes?"

Bastard. "Okay. You've got a point, but—"

"No buts. You're going to relax if it kills us both."

"Relax? How am I supposed to relax?"

Conall pulled her close and began to kiss her neck, his

hands sliding over her body.

"You didn't answer my question, Viking."

"Yes, I did," he muttered against her neck.

Bastard. "So this is your plan?"

"Pretty much. You got a problem with that?" He slid his hands between her thighs and Miki braced her hands against the sides of the tub. God, the things this man did to her. "Miki?"

Christ, she was panting. *When did that start happening?* "What?"

She felt him smile against her flesh. "You didn't answer my question."

Bastard.

℗

Conall snatched the door open and three of his Pack jumped back. "What?"

"Uh..." Billy Dunwich was the only one brave enough to speak in the face of his scowl. "We were just checking on—"

"When we're ready, we'll be down. Until then just wait." He slammed the door in Billy's face. Zach, true to his word, had sent eight of his best wolves to escort Conall and Miki back home. They were even taking a later flight to ensure the whole group would fly together. But until then, he didn't want anything interrupting him and Miki. And he meant *anything.*

He turned and looked at the woman he loved. He didn't even hide the smile on his face. With Miki he didn't have to. She leaned against the desecrated dresser, wearing nothing but one of his T-shirts. It reached to the middle of her calves. "I see."

"You see what?"

"You. You're a closet Alpha."

"I'm a what?"

"You heard me. You're a closet Alpha. You don't really wanna be in charge, but you love to order people around and scare the shit out of them. You're probably only friends with Zach because he doesn't scare easy. Most likely because he's not the brightest bulb in the batch."

Zach was a lot brighter than Miki would ever give him credit for, but other than that she'd hit it all right on the head. The woman absolutely amazed him.

"Is that right?" Conall walked toward her and immediately she began to back away. He watched her nipples get hard under his T-shirt and he listened to her labored breathing. "What else have you figured out about me?"

"You clearly like to stalk me around this hotel room."

"Aw, Miki-baby, don't say that. I'd stalk you anywhere." She laughed and he backed her up to the bed. When her knees hit the mattress, she held her hand up.

"Stay!"

He stopped and watched her.

"I've got to get ready for...uh...ya know...that thing I've gotta do."

Well, he'd wanted her relaxed.

"We've got three hours before your *dissertation*." He nuzzled her outstretched hand until she gave a little moan, then he sucked her middle finger into his mouth.

"You, Viking..." *Christ, is she panting?* "...are a very bad influence."

Miki looked up at him with those big, beautiful brown eyes of hers. "You know," she whispered desperately, "if I start running now I can be back at Sara's by tomorrow night. Afternoon if I don't get stopped by the cops."

"You'll never make it in those shoes." Amazing. The woman faced down lions, hyenas, wolves. Beings that could rip her apart limb from limb. But four puffed-up professors were making her unhinged.

She tugged on her jacket again. "I hate dressing like this. I feel like an idiot."

"Maybe. But you look like a total hottie." *Especially* with those shoes. She ended up wearing the five-inch fuck-me pumps with her prim-and-proper business suit.

"Where's everybody?" she asked, probably not really caring where the Pack might be at the moment.

"I have them around the building."

He brushed her hair out of her eyes, then let his palm rest against her cheek. She didn't push him away. She let him get close. It was the best feeling in the world.

"This is just great. My throat's sore." She sighed and muttered to herself, "Who knew I was a screamer?"

It took all his strength not to drop to his knees and bury his head between her legs right then and there. The beauty of it all was how Miki had no idea what a compliment she'd given him. He did love this woman. How could he not? She was so insane.

She nervously glanced back at the room. Conridge stepped out and motioned to Miki. "I guess this is it."

Conall tugged on her jacket and she looked at him. "You're going to be great, Miki."

"You sure about that, Viking?"

"Positive. And as you know my people are never wrong."

"You know, the Vikings were quite influential—"

He cut her off. "Miki. Go. I'll be here when you come out."

"Right here? You promise?"

He stepped back, leaned against the wall, and then crouched down. "I'll be right here. I promise."

She braved a smile and then headed off toward Conridge. He watched her disappear into the classroom, the door closing soundly behind her.

ॐ

Miki figured they'd asked her questions for about two-and-a-half hours before they felt she had proven herself. Conridge, of course, was the toughest of the professors. But Miki figured she would be and had been ready for it. In fact, she had been ready for all of them. She'd been confident, poised and on point with everything. Even when she screwed up, she made the professors laugh and they let her off the hook.

It seemed Angie and Sara had been right. Bartender-Miki apparently was the way to go because Normal-Miki would have been crying by now.

When she walked out of the classroom, Conall was crouched against the wall exactly where she'd left him. She got the feeling the man hadn't moved. Like he'd promised. She was so startled it took her a second to realize one of the professors was congratulating her. She tore her eyes away from her Viking and finished off her thank-yous.

Once the other professors were gone, Conridge shook her hand. "I knew you'd be fantastic."

"Thanks."

"I'm going to my office. I've got to get out of these clothes. Stop by before you leave with your burly friend."

"Yes, ma'am."

She watched Conridge walk off. Then she turned and faced Conall. He stood and took several steps toward her.

"Well?"

She'd planned to just say "I'm done. Let's go get something to eat." Maybe even give him a thumbs-up. But the way he was looking at her...like he really cared how she did. Like he really wanted to know and he really wanted her to do well, that made her feel...well...special.

Before she knew what she was doing, she'd dropped everything, even her precious briefcase-covered laptop and charged over to him, launching herself into his arms.

"I fucking nailed it!"

Conall held her tight. "I knew you would, Miki-baby. I had no doubts."

She pulled back slightly. "They already told me they were definitely signing off on all my paperwork. They didn't see a reason to make me wait to tell me. I'm going to be *Doctor* Kendrick. Me. How fuckin' cool is that?"

Conall laughed and squeezed her. "We're celebrating."

"Not in these clothes, I'm not." He still held her so they were eye to eye. "Down, Thor." She pointed to the floor. He let her slide down his body and immediately her breath caught. She had absolutely no control around him, but she shook it off. She couldn't get all entangled with him now. They'd done enough illicit activity in the biotech school. "Where's the backpack?"

He grabbed it from the floor and handed it to her. She pulled jeans, sweatshirt, and her steel-toe Docs out of it.

"Can't you keep on the shoes?" He was practically begging.

"Dude, I can't even walk in these things."

"Keep them on and you won't have to walk long." He took a step toward her and she backed up.

Miki's face got hot. "Back off, Viking."

"Come on. For me?"

"No." And just like that, his eyes shifted and he growled. She would have tried to run, but she wasn't going anywhere in these shoes. So she let him pick her up and dump her over his shoulder.

"You son of a bitch! Put me down!"

"You do know that I *am* a son of a bitch. Literally."

She knew he was heading toward the bathroom at the end of the hallway in the hopes of having his dirty way with her. The thought had her tingling from the top of her scalp to the tips of her toes.

He kicked open the bathroom door and walked inside. Lifting her up and gently dropping her to the floor, he grabbed the handful of clothes she still had in her hand and tossed them onto the row of sinks. Then he leaned into her, pinning her against the wall. "I do like when you wear these shoes, Mik. I don't have to crouch as much."

"Are you implying I'm short?"

"I'm not implying anything." He pushed the jacket off her shoulders and kissed her neck. "You are short."

She barked out a laugh and punched his shoulder. "Thank you very much."

He reached down and tugged her skirt up. He gave a combination growl-moan in her ear. "God, woman. You're wearing garters again. What are trying to do to me?"

She reached up and wrapped her arms around his neck.

"Make you crazy."

"You get your kicks that way, don't you?"

"No. I just want you to miss me when I'm gone."

She needed to prepare herself for the inevitable. When Sara's birthday was over, Miki and Conall would both go their separate ways. She wanted to be ready for that. She promised herself she wouldn't become attached. She would keep that promise.

But when Conall pulled away, the expression on his face shocked her. He looked angry. Viking angry. "And where the hell do you think you're going?"

Okay. He wasn't being rational, but come on. Miss her when she was gone? She wasn't going anywhere. Not if he had anything to say about it. And, as far as he was concerned, he had *everything* to say about it. She wasn't leaving him. Not now. Not ever. He loved her. And he couldn't imagine one second of his life without her.

"I just assumed—"

"Well, you assumed wrong. You're not going anywhere."

"I don't like to be ordered around, Conall. And I never promised you anything."

He stepped back from her. He had to. She was in heat. That's why he hadn't been able to keep his hands off her in the hallway. Well, that and the fact she looked so fucking good in those shoes.

He took a deep breath. "You're crazy about me, why don't you just admit it?"

Okay. Where the hell did that come from? That wasn't what he meant to say. And it was definitely the last thing she wanted to hear.

Her eyes narrowed and she pushed past him. "Oh really? *I'm* crazy about *you*?"

"Miki—"

"No. No. I just want to make sure we have the order of worship down correctly."

This was getting bad and he was having a hard time concentrating with her smelling like that. All he could think about was bending her over the sink and fucking her stupid.

"I didn't mean—"

"You know, I'm glad we're getting this out now before we get back to Sara's house, and we give her and Angelina the wrong impression."

"What the fuck do they have to do with anything?"

"Well, they said to give you a try—and that's exactly what I did."

She aimed that one to hurt. Aimed it to cut out his heart and leave it on the ground so she could stomp on it with her Docs.

At first, he didn't say anything. Simply stared at her. Then he pushed her change of clothes at her. "Get dressed. The Pack is waiting."

She snatched the clothes out of his hand and practically ripped her business suit off and put her regular clothes on. When done, she moved to the bathroom door and snatched it open. But Conall's big hand was there slamming it back.

"Wait."

"Why?"

He was so close to her. His body almost, but not quite touching hers. "Because we're not done."

"We're done because we never started."

Miki pulled the bathroom door open and this time he let her. She marched out into the hallway, Conall right behind her.

"What exactly are you scared of, Miki? It's clearly not me. So what is it?"

"We are not about to have one of those bullshit conversations about feelings."

She retrieved her backpack, shoved her business clothes inside it, and slung it over her shoulder. She took her computer bag and placed that over her other shoulder then headed toward the stairs.

"This conversation is over, Conall."

She walked off. She was about twenty feet from the stairs when she heard him growl. Not his usual "You're getting on my nerves, Miki" growl either. Something else altogether. She turned and saw that he'd shifted. Not parts of him. All of him. For the first time since the night of the Pride fight, she saw Conall the wolf. No wonder he'd been pissed about the golden. No way could that little pup be confused with the powerful predator in front of her.

Conall shook off his clothes and then he charged her. Teeth bared. Hackles up. With a tiny squeak that didn't sound anything like her, Miki dropped to her knees, her arms over her head. She waited for impact but there was none. She looked up to see that Conall had sailed right over her and right over the stair railing.

"Holy shit! *Conall!*" She dropped her bags and charged over to the railing. She saw him hit two hyenas on the stairs, knocking them down half a flight. But there were six more and they were all looking at her.

Miki didn't even think about it. She ran.

Chapter Eighteen

Conall didn't know what happened. One minute he was arguing with the crazy woman he secretly called "wife" and the next he was wolf and making mad dashes over railings.

As he sunk his teeth into a throat, he briefly wondered what happened to his Pack. Then he heard them. Growling. Snarling. Fighting. It sounded as if they were kicking some ass, too, but there were so many of the hyenas. As soon as he destroyed one, another two were on his back. Mostly females, vicious beyond anything he'd ever experienced before.

Then he remembered Miki. Last he saw she was ducking and covering. Had she actually thought he'd hurt her? He was the least of her problems.

Still, Conall wasn't worried *about* Miki as much as he was worried *for* her. Because the one thing he knew about his woman—she could take care of herself.

Miki charged down the stairs on the opposite side of the building. She heard the hyenas coming for her. They had the most disturbing howl she'd ever experienced, like brutal, mocking laughter. She had to force her body to move. All she really wanted to do was hide in a corner and cry. Anything to block out that sound.

She took two steps at a time, and stopped on the second floor, running down the hallway until she hit Conridge's office. By then they were snapping at her heels. She had barely enough time to get into Conridge's office and slam the door. She held her body against it and could feel them throwing themselves at the hard wood.

Seconds later Conridge was beside her, adding her weight against the door. The woman had thankfully changed clothes. She now wore a pullover sweater, jeans and running shoes. It seemed she would need the running shoes.

"What the hell?"

"Hyenas," Miki panted out, her mind scrambling for what to do next.

Even as Conridge locked the door, the two women continued to keep their bodies against it. But it wouldn't last much longer. With every hit the hinges became weaker.

"We've got to get out of here." Conridge's eyes began to search the room for some escape. She didn't have a window, but she had a vent. But Miki wasn't about to get trapped in that with hyenas on her ass.

Her amped-up Stop the Bark tragically still sat in her backpack with her house keys, and there was no way to get to it without heading back toward the hyenas. *No way.* Plus she needed to kill these things, not incapacitate them.

"Is there any chance in hell you have a gun?"

"Bottom drawer on the left." When Miki just stared at her, "I don't have claws, Ms. Kendrick. So I had to find other ways to protect myself. You know the world does not revolve around the Magnus Pack. The Van Holtz Pack has its own enemies."

Fair enough. Miki left Conridge to hold the door while she tore through her drawer. She almost cried when she found two loaded Sig Sauer P239s. The P239s were compact and fit her hand pretty well. Both were .357s, so there were only seven rounds per magazine but, bless her, Conridge had extra clips already filled with ammo. She liked this woman more and more.

Miki stuck one gun in the back of her jeans and several already loaded clips in her front jeans pocket. Then she stood in front of the door and dropped to her knees. She leveled the weapon in both hands and watched the door as the hyenas on the other side relentlessly pounded away trying to get to her. She watched the movement of the door. The way it buckled and where it buckled. She listened to the sounds they made when they made contact with the wood. Then she waited for that "click" inside her head.

Conridge watched her but didn't say anything. When Miki finally spoke, she was ready.

"Move."

Conridge took several quick steps to the side and covered her ears. Miki took one more second to clear her mind and body and then she shot three rounds through the door. She heard yelps of pain and surprise and then nothing.

After a minute, Conridge stepped forward and listened at the door.

"I don't hear anything." She put her hand on the doorknob. "Be ready," was all she said before she eased the door open and glanced into the hallway.

"Holy shit."

Miki looked at her professor. It was the first time she ever heard the woman utter anything except "hell" and the occasional "damn".

"You're a hell of shot, Ms. Kendrick."

Miki stood and went to the door. She pulled it completely open, the gun out but at an angle so she didn't accidentally kill someone important. There were three hyenas dead on the floor. Miki frowned.

"There were six on the stairs that Conall wasn't fighting," she whispered. She pulled the other gun out of her waistband. She offered it to Conridge, but the older woman shook her head. "I'm not the best shot." She gazed at the hyena corpses. "Not like you."

Miki shrugged. She'd been smart enough to learn to shoot with both hands. Amazing what you can get done when you're under house arrest.

She had both guns out and low at her sides. Then she stepped into the hallway. She saw them silently moving at her from both directions from the corners of her eyes. She raised both weapons and fired.

Two went down immediately. One kept coming. So she turned and fired, brain and skull splattering the walls.

"We need to get into Craig's lab."

"I've got keys." Conridge grabbed her purse and put it over her shoulder. Miki re-traced her steps to head back up to the third floor where she could find Craig's lab, Conridge right behind her.

She thought about Conall. She could hear the Pack fighting outside the building. The wolves would be outnumbered. Hyena Clans could have up to forty members. The thought of anything happening to Conall almost sent her skidding into full-blown panic. But freaking out now wouldn't help him or her.

She knew what Craig kept in his lab. She'd put it there herself. She knew what it could do. Hell, she'd invented it. And if she had time, she'd probably realize that using her invention was the dumbest thing she could do. But she had the feeling she didn't have time to come up with anything else. Time was something they no longer had.

She walked onto the third floor and stopped cold. Leucrotta. He had only shifted partially and was on top of one of the wolves. A female. She was out cold and it seemed that Leucrotta had been sniffing her.

He looked at Miki and smiled. An unbelievably sharp row of small but deadly fangs revealed. He stood and shifted almost completely back to human...except for the teeth. He walked toward her and she raised both guns.

Conridge was behind her. "He's human."

"So?"

"You kill him now, he stays human." Well, that would be difficult to explain to the cops. And she wasn't sure she was ready to actually blow a human away. That actually might bother her...at least for a little while.

"She's right. You don't want to kill me now, Miki." His voice was like a hiss. The sound went across her skin and raised the hair on the back of her neck. If she had been wolf, her hackles would have been standing straight up right across her back. "Besides, don't you like my little congratulations party for you, Dr. Kendrick?"

"Are you working with the Pride?"

"That'll be a cold day in hell." He kept moving toward her and she could feel Conridge's hand gripping the back of her shirt. The woman was having a minor freak out.

"So then what do you want?"

He shrugged. "How should I know? This fight belongs to the females. They tell me what to do and I do it because I like doing it. And they told me to tear your Pack apart and to feed on your entrails."

Miki snorted. "Melodramatic bullshit." Then she lowered the gun and pulled the trigger. Twice. Leucrotta went down screaming. Both knees blown out.

She heard Conridge gasp behind her. "Oh, my."

Miki glanced at the woman over her shoulder. "You said not to kill him. You didn't say anything about his knees."

಍

One of them ripped a good chunk out of Conall's thigh with its claws and he roared in anger. Especially when he felt the poison began to seep into his blood stream.

Fuckers.

He tore the bitch's throat out and flipped it up and over his back.

He was lucky. The whole Clan wasn't there. With a full Clan, he'd have been dead. But there were still twelve left. The five he'd already killed were lying in the building. Another three were lying on the ground at his feet. He could only hope that Miki grabbed the SUV keys out of his discarded jeans and made it to the parking lot where he'd left it. He could only hope she would be safe. That was all he cared about now.

Another set of jaws locked onto the back of his neck. Billy Dunwich tackled the hyena and ripped its leg off as he hit the ground. Conall faced another one and that's when he smelled her. With her going into heat, it came to him a lot sooner.

"Hi. Am I interrupting anything important?"

They all turned to look at her. Conall gave a warning bark. She needed to move her ass. The hyenas wouldn't be distracted for long. She just surprised them with her sudden appearance.

But it was the look in her eye that caught his attention. And the fact she had her hands behind her back. Plus she was standing just a little too cutesy for the Miki Kendrick he knew.

With one leg cocked slightly in toward her other leg, her head tilted. Like a little girl.

Then it hit him. She was *trying* to look nonthreatening. But why? He decided not to wait to find out. He looked at the other wolves and, as one, they turned and ran.

Miki had their attention and it was damn scary. Those cold animal eyes staring at her. Sizing her up. Wondering what bits to eat first. But she needed Conall and the Pack to move. Now. But if she warned them then the hyenas would know, too. She knew from Sara that shifters could understand everything. They thought, heard, and saw as if they were still human.

Then, suddenly, Conall and the Pack hightailed it out of there. She didn't know what clued him in, but she wasn't going to worry about it. A few of the hyenas watched the Pack run. They weren't a stupid breed. In fact, they were the exact opposite. They would know something was up, so she had to move now or lose her opportunity.

She raised her two guns. The hyenas stared at her for a moment and then began...laughing? It took every ounce of inner strength she had not to curl up into the fetal position and start crying for her grandmother. But, her grandmother had been a strong, mean woman and she would have told Miki to get her shit together anyway.

But Miki knew what they were laughing at. She didn't have enough bullets in those two guns to take out all the Clan members in front of her. She may kill a few, but the rest would tear her apart.

She already knew that.

"Now!" The female wolf that Leucrotta had been sniffing stepped out of the shadows and tossed a mason jar, filled with the clear liquid Miki had created so many years ago, into the air. Miki raised one of the guns and fired. The jar exploded over the hyenas and, within seconds, flames covered their bodies.

A chemical flame that as soon as it touched the fur on the first hyena spread over the entire body within seconds. As the hyena tried to shake it off, it got too close to another Clan member and the flame spread. That was the beauty of her concoction, and one of the reasons her government had tried to get her to produce it for them. It wasn't like regular fire. It almost took on a life of its own, jumping from victim to victim as long as they were in a ten-foot range. It only went after flesh, fur, or skin, too. The buildings, trees, even the grass would be largely unaffected except for a few burn marks she never could figure out how to get rid of before she stopped working on the experiments all together.

The hyenas began to go up in flames as the wolf female tossed the other bottle on the opposite side and Miki shot that one as well. Then the female lobbed one to the right and left of the hyenas. Miki shot all of them without any problems. It was like skeet shooting. She only needed four bullets for that.

A ring of fire surrounded the hyenas. A fire that wouldn't spread out but in. Once again, a little extra "thing" about her concoction. By the time the fire department showed up, they'd find a pile of hyena ash and a fire that would go out in about five more minutes without water or a fire extinguisher.

"Go!" The female took off running. Two hyenas, untouched by the flame, charged Miki. She fired both guns. One crumpled on impact. The other flipped head over tail.

Miki ran. Two hyenas still on her ass. Unfortunately, they hadn't been close enough to the fire to get hurt. If she stopped to shoot, they'd take her down. She saw Conridge pull up in a minivan. A typical mom car. Thankfully it had automated doors that slid open at her approach. Miki dove for it but hyena teeth grabbed onto her calf.

She had on jeans but those strong jaws went right through to the flesh beneath. "Motherfucker!" Miki kicked with her free foot, but the hyena wouldn't let go. It yanked and dragged her out of the van, flipping her to her back. That's when she fired. She couldn't get a clean head shot without shooting herself in the foot, so she shot it in the ass. It yelped and danced away. The second one came for her. She aimed the gun, her finger about to pull the trigger. Then suddenly the female who had been helping her shifted back to wolf in mid-flight and took the hyena down. She twisted its neck and snapped it.

Miki struggled to stand, but strong hands grabbed her from behind and lifted her to her feet. She looked over her shoulder and frowned. She'd assumed it was Conall but it was another Pack member.

"Where's Conall?" He didn't answer her, but lifted her and threw her into the van. The rest of the Pack, some human and some still wolf, followed in behind her. He slammed the door and Conridge moved. The woman drove like she taught. Dangerously.

"Wait! We're not leaving without Conall!" She had the guns and they all knew she'd use them in a heartbeat.

"He's back here." One of the females motioned to her.

Miki clamored over the seats and around the Pack members, doing her best to ignore the pain in her calf. She could hear sirens blaring as cops headed their way. They'd probably gotten out just in time.

As she stumbled to the back, she found Conall in the rear boot. He was still wolf. His shoulder torn open. His struggle to breathe obvious.

"It's poison," the female next to her explained. "We need to get him someplace safe."

Conridge spoke from the front, "You'll come to Van Holtz territory. You'll be safe there. And our doctor can help him."

Miki slid into the back with Conall. She petted his head.

"Miki? Is that cool with you?" Miki looked up. The female, Patty was her name maybe, stared at her. Waiting for an answer. It took Miki a second to realize the Pack waited for her decision. When Zach and Sara weren't around, Conall was in charge. With Conall down that meant the next strongest was in charge. She suddenly realized that was her.

"Yeah. Yeah. That's cool."

She focused back on Conall, running her hands over his flanks, avoiding the bloody wound on his shoulder.

"Conall. Can you hear me?"

He rubbed his snout against her arm. "I'll take that as a yes." She searched around her for something to wrap his wound. "Baby, can you shift back for me?"

He whined and she took that as a no. At least not yet.

"That's okay, baby. That's okay." She grabbed a kid-sized bottle of water from a box lying next to Conall's head and a small T-shirt she found. She tore the shirt into strips and drenched the strips in water.

She wiped the wound with the wet cloth, sniffed it, but couldn't recognize what they'd used on him.

Taking him to a hospital was out. Taking him to the vet equally so. She could only hope the Van Holtz Pack would help.

She leaned in close to him. "Conall, will you be able to hold on for a bit?" He licked her arm. "Okay. Good. We're going someplace safe."

He licked her face. "Don't worry, baby. I've got ya, okay?" He made a soft sound and she rubbed the fur at the back of his neck. "I've got ya."

Chapter Nineteen

Conall forced his eyes open, wincing at the pain in his head. He glanced around and realized he was in the back seat of some vehicle he didn't recognize. He looked down. He was human. His shoulder hurt. The poison had taken hold and traveled around his system like a flame on gasoline. But his body fought it. He could feel the fever coming on. This would definitely get worse before it got better.

But he didn't care. Not really. He needed to know if Miki was safe. Was she alive? He heard doors opening and felt hands on his body. He tried to fight, but he didn't have strength left. He heard grunts as they hoisted him up and then he was moving.

Miki limped behind the wolves that had Conall. Her leg was killing her, but not from poison. If she'd been poisoned, she'd be dead by now. She wasn't wolf and she would never be able to fight the effects. Conall was wolf. But whether he would live or not, well, no one could give her an answer on that.

When they arrived at Van Holtz territory, she was surprised at the size of Conridge's home. It was huge but extremely modest. She liked that it wasn't fancy. She saw Conridge's husband at the front door. He was even more gorgeous than his picture. A typical wolf, too. Tall, broad and devastatingly handsome. His relief at seeing his wife was blinding. He swept her into his arms and lifted the woman off her feet, hugging her close against his body.

Miki thought about Conall and she felt that tightness around her heart again. The pain worse than the one in her leg. *What if he dies?* She stopped the thought. Of all the things she tortured herself with on a daily basis, this couldn't be one of them. She'd never survive it.

They carried Conall into the house and Conridge motioned for them to go up to the next floor. Miki went to follow, but Conridge grabbed her arm.

"No, you don't. I want to take a look at that leg."

"I'm not leaving him."

Conridge pulled her toward the back of the house. "Of course not. But the wolves have him now. Niles called in one of their own. He's a physician. Give him some time with Conall. And while they do that, we'll deal with you."

Miki allowed Conridge to drag her to their spotless kitchen. Funny, Sara's kitchen was spotless because apparently none of them used it. Conridge's kitchen was spotless because someone in her family was obsessive compulsive.

"Don't take this the wrong way, but drop your pants." Miki would have laughed if she had it in her. But she didn't. She dropped her pants and Conridge gently forced her into a chair.

Conridge was on her knees, pulling Miki's leg up to examine her wound when Niles Van Holtz walked into the kitchen. He took one look at his wife and raised an eyebrow.

"Don't go there," Conridge warned without even looking at the man.

"I didn't say a word." His gaze shifted to Miki. "Have you eaten?"

"I'm not hungry."

"So no it is." He went to a row of cabinets and pulled out a pot, a sauté pan, and fresh pasta from the stainless-steel refrigerator.

"He's ignoring me." Miki didn't even recognize her own voice. There was no life in it. And until Conall recovered, *if* he recovered, she'd be dead inside.

"Of course he's ignoring you. He's wolf. That's what they do when they don't like what they hear." Conridge cleaned off the wound, wiped it down with mercurochrome, and wrapped it in a clean white bandage. "It's going to hurt like hell, but it will heal."

"Thank you."

Conridge looked up into Miki's face. She wasn't sure what the woman saw but her face softened to the point where Miki barely recognized her. She actually looked kind of pretty. "I know you're scared, Miki. But they're doing all they can for Conall. He's wolf, he'll fight."

Miki nodded as Conridge got to her feet. "Let me get you some clothes." She spoke to her husband. "And I'm stealing a few things from you for the rest of her Pack." Miki didn't bother telling them they weren't her Pack. She was too emotionally drained.

"I'll be right back." Conridge squeezed Miki's shoulder and walked out.

Miki watched Van Holtz at the stove. She was impressed. The man seemed to know what he was doing. And whatever he was creating did smell good.

"You'll be safe until morning. By then we'll know if Víga-Feilan will..." He stopped and looked at her over his shoulder.

"Survive?"

"I wouldn't worry too much. He looks...well, *really* strong. And the fever has already taken hold."

"Fever?"

"It's how our bodies fight. The fever can last up to twenty-four hours. And you never know what will happen when you're going through it. Sometimes nothing. Sometimes you shift a thousand times in twenty minutes. And sometimes you start flipping out. It's a crapshoot."

"I should be with him."

"After you eat." Van Holtz dumped some sautéed pasta onto a dish, added some extra cheese, grabbed a fork, and plopped it down in front of Miki. "You have to eat it. I usually charge fifteen bucks for that dish in my restaurant."

It smelled great and her stomach suddenly roared to life. Taking a deep breath, she took the fork he held out to her and sampled the food. It tasted as good as it smelled.

"Thank you."

He patted her on the shoulder then walked away. She ate while he cleaned up his kitchen. An obsessive-compulsive wolf. *Odd.*

As Miki took the last bite she could manage, a girl walked into the kitchen in shorts and a T-shirt, a soccer ball under her arm. "I'm back from practice, Papa."

The girl reached up on tiptoe to kiss her father.

"How did you do?" he asked.

"Fine. But the rest of the team is holding me back." The girl turned and looked at Miki. "Hello."

"Hi."

"Who are you?"

"I'm Miki."

"Kendrick?"

Miki blinked. "Yeah."

"I read your dissertation." Suddenly the girl looked just like her mother. "I found flaws." The girl walked out of the room.

Miki stared at Van Holtz and he shrugged in answer. "She takes after her mother."

Conridge pushed the kitchen door open, but she was yelling over her shoulder. "I said do your homework this minute, mister. And don't you dare bare your fangs at me!" She came in with a pair of sweatpants and a long-sleeved tee. "Damn wolf children."

Conridge handed Miki the clothes. Without even thinking about the fact that Van Holtz stood right there, she changed into them.

Just as she finished pulling the tee over her head, Billy Dunwich stuck his head into the kitchen. "Miki, we need you."

Miki moved. Ignoring the pain in her leg, she followed after Dunwich who was now wearing only a pair of jeans. He took her up the stairs and to a door. She could hear snarling and snapping, so she pushed past him and threw the door open. Conall as wolf was out of control. She could see the whites of his eyes as he spun in a circle and snapped at anyone who got too close to him. The one she assumed was the Pack doctor had a needle out and stood behind several Van Holtz wolves. The other wolves seemed at a loss on what to do.

She walked into the room. "Conall!" The wolf spun around at the sound of her voice. She sat down on the floor Indian style. "Come here, baby." He ran to her. His shoulder had started bleeding again and he had a pronounced limp. He came to her and dropped in front of her, his head in her lap. He whined and then shuddered. "It's okay, baby. I won't let anyone hurt you." She petted his head and waited until he'd calmed down. She looked up at the doctor. "All right. Do it."

The doctor walked over, crouched down beside them, and quickly shot Conall up with whatever was in the needle. She glanced up at Dunwich. "Get him up on the bed." Conall's Pack lifted him up and placed him back on the bed.

"Everybody out."

"Are you sure?"

She nodded at Dunwich's question. "Yeah. I'll be fine."

The wolves left. The doctor, the last to go. "You'll have to clean off that wound again, but that shot should keep him calm. He'll probably wake up, though, while in the throes of the fever. I'll be taking care of the other wolves who were injured tonight, so I'll be here if you need me."

"Thanks."

The doctor walked out, closing the door behind him.

Miki glanced around the room. It was a huge bedroom with an adjoining bathroom. She was thankful for that. She didn't want to leave Conall at all. She never wanted to leave Conall. And that thought absolutely terrified her.

Chapter Twenty

Conall felt cold. Freezing cold. He pried his eyes open and looked around the room. He had no idea where he was. But even worse, he didn't see Miki. Where was Miki? He needed to make sure she was okay.

"Miki?" He tried to sit up but his head was pounding.

"Hey. Hey. No, you don't, Viking." He felt her warm hands on his chest, pushing him back down on to the mattress. "You're not going anywhere yet."

"Safe? Are you safe?"

"We're both safe, baby. Everything's cool. Just sleep."

He grabbed her hand and pulled her close. "Stay with me, Mik."

"I'm not going anywhere."

He smiled, his eyes closing. "Promise?"

She chuckled. "Yeah. I promise."

He settled back down into the bed, but he still wouldn't release her hand.

"You're not going to let me go, are you, Viking?"

"I'm never letting you go, Mik. Besides, I'm cold. I need you to warm me up."

She sighed and he felt the bed dip slightly as she got in next to him. "Okay. Okay. Come here."

She pulled him close, laying his head against her chest. He wrapped his arms around her and held her tight. She kissed the top of his head as her arms wrapped around his shoulders.

"You smell good," he rasped. "You're in heat."

She laughed softly. "Christ, Conall, get some sleep."

Knowing she was safe, he allowed himself to relax. She smelled so good and he felt incredibly soothed by the heat coming off her body. The last thing he remembered was her hands running through his hair.

Miki brushed Conall's hair out of his face. He slept again. For hours he'd been waking up, worried about whether she was safe or not. It almost overwhelmed her, his constant concern for her. She'd always had the love and protection of women. Her mother and grandmother. Sara and Angelina. But never of men. Most men found her either overwhelming or a little scary. Even Craig and the guys seemed to have a healthy fear of her.

But Conall. Conall was different. Did he actually care about her or was it just the fever? How the hell was she supposed to know? She knew science. Math. And some history. She knew how to make an amazing martini and she had a decent roundhouse kick. That was it. Anything to do with people and actual emotions, she was totally at a loss.

Miki kissed Conall's forehead again and settled down next to him. She was so tired. Not surprising with everything that had happened in the past few hours. But with a little nap, just a few minutes, she'd be right as rain.

She closed her eyes and let sleep take her.

He was having the best dream. One of those hot dreams with Miki that he'd been having since he met her. He was enjoying this dream too because she smelled so good. She was in heat.

He was behind her, his arms wrapped tight around her waist. He nuzzled her neck and licked it. She sighed softly and snuggled back into him. "My wolf."

"All yours, baby."

Her hand gripped his thigh. "Make me come, wolf."

Oh, yeah. What a *great* dream. He slid his hand down her stomach and under her panties, easing his fingers between her thighs and over her clit. Her body jerked and she gave a little moan as two of his fingers entered her pussy. She was already wet. Wet and hot. She gripped his hand and pushed his fingers deeper.

He smiled and he slowly finger fucked her. She moaned again, her tight ass writhing against his cock. It had already been hard, now it was on fire. It wanted to be deep inside her. As deep as his fingers were. Deeper. He ran his thumb over her clit and she gasped, her head falling back against his shoulder. "God, Conall." He loved when she said his name with that sexy voice of hers. He *felt* her voice all over his body.

The pad of his thumb circled her clit and her fingers dug into his hand. Her body tightened. He licked the back of her neck again. "Miki?"

She pushed herself back into him, her body beginning to shake. "Do it, Conall. Please."

"You sure, baby?"

"Please," she asked again. And he knew it was a dream because Miki would have kicked him in the nuts by now. Not begged him.

He extended his fangs and, turning his head to the side, bit the back of her neck. She gave a little cry but he wasn't sure if it was from the bite or the bone-shaking orgasm she was having. To be honest, he didn't care. As he licked the blood off, he only knew one thing. She was his now. And nothing would ever change that.

At least not here, in his dreams.

Miki was having the most rockin' dream ever. A dream that consisted of one of those screaming orgasms only Conall seemed to have the ability to wring out of her. This time with nothing more than his hands and teeth. In this dream she let him mark her. Practically begged him to, in fact. It felt so right, though. And it was a dream, so she didn't have to be scared or worry about getting hurt. Or about being in love.

She could do anything she wanted here. She pulled his hand out of her and turned in his arms, kissing him deep and slow. Their tongues connecting, sliding, teasing. She felt his dick against her leg. It was hard and hot and all hers. She reached down and gripped it, her thumb sweeping across the head.

Conall growled into her mouth. "God, Miki-baby." His hands took hold of her shirt and pulled it over her head. Her bra went next. Then he was kissing his way down her body as he dragged her sweatpants and panties off. He kissed his way back up, lingering on her breasts. Then her neck. Kissing her mouth again. Taking his time to explore.

His body always felt so good to her. So right next to hers. He moved over her and she felt his dick slide inside her. Her back arched, almost throwing Conall off.

He felt so good inside her. He wasn't wearing a condom and her muscles gripped him tight, pulling him deep. He growled again and she felt it across her body.

His thrusts were slow and deep and she was completely lost in them. Her body rose to meet his, loving the feel of his flesh. Nothing had ever felt so right before.

Before she knew it, an orgasm slammed into her and she gripped Conall to her tight. Then he was coming inside of her. Another orgasm rocked her just after the last one ended. She clamped onto Conall's chest with her teeth and bit down. She tasted blood and, before she knew it, she was licking his wound clean. As both their bodies settled down, she unclamped her teeth and released his flesh, but she held on tight to the man.

"I love you, Viking," she whispered, enjoying her dream moment.

"I love you, Miki-baby." Then her dream man started snoring.

Chapter Twenty-One

Conall woke up when the sun hit his eyes through the window. He felt great. Better than great. That was the cool thing about the fever. If you survived it, you usually felt better than you did before you got hurt.

Miki was in his arms and he relished it. Especially since the last thing he remembered from the night before was having a huge screaming argument with her. But he didn't want to think about that now. He pulled her closer and she sighed softly in her sleep.

As right as this all felt, he knew something was wrong. He just couldn't quite figure out what. He looked down at her. Asleep and as beautiful as always, she was also naked and had her limbs around him. It took him a second, but he realized he was inside her. Inside her without a condom.

Uh-oh.

The pillow behind her head had blood on it. He winced as he gently reached around and touched the back of her neck. Then it was her turn to wince from him touching the wound.

He remembered that the day before she'd been going into heat. He leaned in and sniffed her. Her scent had changed. Which meant only one thing.

He closed his eyes. *She is going to kick my ass.*

She stirred underneath him and he immediately got hard again. Boy, was this bad timing.

Miki stretched, her arms going wide, pushing him off and out of her. She yawned and rubbed her hands over her face. She looked around and then seemed to remember why she was...well, wherever the hell they were.

"Conall?" She turned and looked at him. "Conall? Are you okay?"

"Yeah, Mik. I'm fine." She leaned over him and felt his forehead. Her bare breasts rubbed against his arm and he had the sudden urge to have her again.

"Your fever broke. That's good." She gave him the oddest expression. Then she suddenly launched herself into his arms. He was so startled, he fell back on the bed. He pulled her close and she hugged him tight. "I'm so glad you're okay," she whispered fiercely.

He closed his eyes. Nothing ever felt so right as when this woman was in his arms. And knowing she actually cared about him enough to worry...nothing before had ever made him feel so good.

Miki, clearly not comfortable with showing her emotions, pulled herself out of his arms. She sat on the edge of the bed. "I'm really sorry about yesterday, ya know." She glanced at him, then turned away again. "You took me by surprise. And I never thought you'd want...I just never had..." She shook her head and he saw her smile. "Forget it. We'll talk about this later. Really talk. You and me. Okay?"

But before he could answer her. Before he could tell her the decision had already been made for them, she slid out of bed and headed to the bathroom. "When I'm done, I'll let Van Holtz and the Pack know you're okay."

Christ, they were on another Pack's territory. Well that

explained the strange wolf scent he smelled everywhere.

Conall lay back on the bed and waited. Waited for her to realize what had happened. She probably thought like he first did. That it had been a dream. But he had marked her. She was his. Would be for life. And there would never be another woman for him. Never.

But he knew Miki almost better than he knew himself now. She wasn't going to take this well. She'd feel trapped. And she hated feeling trapped. He was having trouble remembering last night but he knew they'd been caught up in something primal and older than most of the gods. In fact, he was almost positive she'd told him to mark her. Knew what he intended without him actually saying it. The wolf in him wanted her. Knew she was the mate for him. And she was.

Miki could have run yesterday. Taken off with Conridge and never looked back. But she'd faced down a vicious Clan of hyenas to protect him and his Pack mates. She hadn't even been worried about herself. Only him. Those were the actions of a mate. *His* mate.

He heard the toilet flush and Conall counted. "Five. Four. Three. Two—"

"Conall!"

"One." He sighed and waited.

Miki stormed out of the bathroom, wearing only white sweat socks and a really pissed-off look.

"What the fuck is this?" She pointed at the back of her neck. He didn't bother to look. Not when she was standing in front of him naked.

"My mark."

She stared at him. He waited for it. The explosion of anger. The rants. All of it. He knew it was coming.

But it didn't come. Miki just stared at him. Then she silently grabbed her clothes off the floor and returned to the bathroom, quietly closing the door behind her.

Okay. That was *definitely* not the reaction he expected. He expected rage. Rage he knew how to deal with. Whatever she was going through at the moment, they didn't even have a name for.

He got off the bed and pushed the bathroom door open. She had gotten on her shirt and panties but that was it. Now she sat on the edge of the bathtub holding her sweatpants in her hand and staring down at the floor.

"Miki?"

She looked up at him. Her dark eyes glittered in the well-lit bathroom. "You couldn't let me decide for myself, could you?"

This was controlled rage, and this worried him. When she was ranting and raving, he knew she was simply being wacky Miki. But this…this was Miki who blew the head off a lion.

"It wasn't like that, Mik, and you know it."

She sighed. Calmly. He was getting more and more freaked out by the second. "I'm going back to Texas, Conall."

He crouched down next to her, gently laying his hand on her leg. "No." He spoke softly. He wanted her to know she was safe. Safe with him. "Not until we talk about—*ow*!"

She'd punched him. Right in the nose.

"What the hell was that for?"

"*Because you're a lying sack of shit!* That's what that's for!" Yeah. There was the Miki he knew and loved. "I'm going back to Texas and you can't fucking stop me!"

Conall stood, crossed his arms in front of his chest, and blocked the doorway. "No. You're not."

She stared at him. Those big, giant arms, crossed in front of that big, giant chest. His big legs braced apart. He was completely blocking the doorway. Hell, he was completely blocking her. And she didn't like it one damn bit.

"I wasn't asking you, Conall."

"You're not running away from this. From us."

Us? At what point did the booty call turn into an "us".

She dropped her head in her hands in pure frustration. He was making her nuts. "There is no us. There will never be an us."

"Why?"

Okay. Why did that question throw her? "Because."

"Because why?"

Christ, it was like talking to a ten-year-old. "Because I said so."

He smiled. "That the best you can do, Miki-baby?"

"Don't call me that."

"It never bothered you before."

She stood and pulled on the sweatpants. "Well, it bothers me now."

He stepped toward her and she stepped back. "And why is that?" She backed up against the stainless steel sink as he moved in front of her. "Because I usually say that when I'm inside you? When you're coming and screaming my name?"

Okay. Why couldn't she breathe? He was so close and smelled so good. No. This wouldn't do. She needed to go. Somewhere. Anywhere. Away from him. She needed time to think. To analyze. To plan.

"Last night you told me you loved me." *Oh, that he remembered.*

"I was asleep."

"Not too asleep to fuck me."

"Christ, Conall." She wanted to push him away, but she knew she couldn't touch his skin. If she touched him, she'd be lost.

"Tell me you don't care about me, Miki." He leaned in, his mouth so close. "Tell me and maybe I'll believe you."

"I don't care about you." That would have been much more convincing if she hadn't whispered it while staring at his mouth.

His lips were inches from hers. "Liar." Then he was kissing her. His lips on hers, his tongue sliding into her mouth. His hands tangling in her hair. Immediately, her body responded. Her arms went around his neck. Her body pressed into his. And her desire to drop to her knees and take him into her mouth almost overwhelmed her.

He pulled back slightly, but his hands were still in her hair and his upper body still had her trapped against the sink. "Stay with me, Miki."

"I can't think about this right now." Panting. She really had to stop panting.

"Then don't think at all." His mouth captured hers again and she became wet for him. Nipples became hard. All the usual. She had no control around him. None.

When he dropped to his knees, she almost exploded. Why was he doing this to her? She was trying to make it easy on him. Giving him a way out. Why was he torturing her?

Because, idiot, maybe he doesn't want a way out. Okay. Exactly when did that new voice make an entrance in her head?

Conall pulled off her sweatpants and panties and tossed them aside. Then he pushed her legs apart and began to lap at her clit.

"Goddamn it, Conall!" He ignored her. What was it Conridge had said? If they don't like what they hear, they just ignore it. And, clearly, that's what her Viking was doing. But his tongue felt so good. And then he growled. A deep one from low in his chest. It reverberated up and through his tongue, hitting right across her clit and sending Miki spiraling out of control. Nothing, absolutely nothing, had ever felt that good before. She gripped his head in both her hands and held him in place. She loved the feel of his hair against the inside of her thighs. She loved the warmth of his body. She loved the way his hands gripped her ass as he ate her out. She loved all of it. All of him.

The growling, the licking, they all conspired to shove her over the edge. And shove they did. The guttural moan she let out as she climaxed sounded like it was coming from somewhere else. From someone else altogether.

While her body still shook from her climax, Conall picked her up and placed her on the sink. Then he was inside her. It seemed she wasn't the only one out of control. She wrapped her legs around his waist and held on as he gripped her hips with his hands and claimed her body. Every time he took her it felt better than the time before.

Her head fell back and Conall's mouth sucked on her throat. She loved this man. She knew she did. But she was scared to death. She'd always assumed that she'd be alone forever. She'd simply hoped that no matter where Angie and Sara ended up, they'd always have a place for her at Thanksgiving dinner.

But the Viking...

He'd marked and mated her without a backward glance. And she'd told him to. She thought that had just been an astounding dream. An astounding *wet* dream. Now she knew it had really happened. Half asleep or not, they'd connected on a level she never thought existed between people. Now, according to Sara, she was "his". And her fast-moving brain simply wasn't ready to handle that.

Of course, that didn't stop her body from completely exploding as Conall slammed into her. She bit into his unwounded shoulder as his hot seed shot into her. That's when she realized he wasn't wearing a condom and that he hadn't been the night before. Apparently, they were so much a couple now condoms were optional.

And as soon as her body stopped shaking from her climax, she was going to say something about this.

"Hey, Conall. You here?" A male voice. Probably Dunwich. He seemed the only one brave enough to deal with Conall when he was with her. "Van Holtz got your stuff back from the SUV and the school hallway. A few of the cops handling the case are Pack. So we should be cool."

Miki tensed and tried to pull away, but Conall wouldn't let her go. He held her to him as he got his voice back. "Good. Thanks. We'll be out in a few."

"Uh...yeah. Sure. Okay."

Miki rolled her eyes as she heard that amused sound in Dunwich's voice. *Schmuck.*

Conall kissed Miki's forehead. No way was he letting her go. Now he understood why Zach couldn't leave Sara alone. Because when you find that right one, you don't want to let her go. Even when she was a pain in the ass. Of course, Conall was willing to overlook Miki's ability to be a pain in the ass as long as she kept having those orgasms that almost snapped his cock in two.

"We'll talk about this later, okay? Just don't make any

decisions now."

"Conall—"

"Let's just get back to the den, okay?"

She wanted to argue. She wanted to tell him this wasn't right. He could see it on her face. But he wasn't going to let her. Instead, he'd get her back to the house and then he'd fuck her into submission again and again until she finally got the message she was his and he was hers. Forever.

Yeah. That worked as a plan.

He pulled out of her and was surprised she didn't say anything about his lack of condom. He knew it was no longer necessary, but she still didn't. And he wasn't going to say anything about the pregnancy until he convinced her they should be together. He didn't need anything else freaking her out. He was coaxing a high-strung mare. Scare her off now and she'd hightail that fine ass right back to Texas. If she were going to accept the fact that she was his, he'd have to play this cool. Well, as cool as he could when just her touch on his shoulder made his whole body throb.

Chapter Twenty-Two

He thought the Van Holtz Pack would toss them out as soon as he could walk. Man, had he been wrong. Instead Niles Van Holtz made them all breakfast. The most amazing waffles he'd ever tasted, eggs, bacon, coffee, orange juice, the works. The man was a genius of the kitchen.

He sat next to Miki as she and Conridge talked about how the university management had already begun to successfully cover up the hyena attacks by dismissing them as a pack of wild dogs that found their way onto campus and then proceeded to wreck havoc. The fire Miki started disappeared so fast that it barely got a mention. And no one had any idea what happened to Professor Leucrotta. Conall forced himself not to react when he heard about the man's knees, although his Pack seemed to be quietly disturbed.

It seemed his mate had done serious damage. To protect him. To protect his Pack. He kept thinking "She didn't walk away. She didn't walk away." And she could have. She so easily could have.

He looked at his Pack. They all feared her. Even the Van Holtz Pack. And now that they knew she was pregnant, now that they could smell it on her, they were waiting to see what she would do if she realized. Even Niles Van Holtz kept looking at him as if to say "Welcome to my world, buddy."

As if on cue, Conridge's kids stormed into the room. The boys were typical wolf pups. Loud, boisterous, with sharp teeth. The girl was different. She didn't seem more than twelve or thirteen, but she moved slowly. Paced herself. She wasn't doglike at all, but she smelled like wolf. She would be Pack leader one day. And she already knew it.

She walked serenely after her brothers, heading toward the kitchen door leading to the hallway. But suddenly she stopped and looked straight at Miki.

"You weren't pregnant last night, were you?"

The entire room of people froze. If Conall didn't know better, he would have sworn that the entire universe had frozen. That, like them, the universe wanted to see what Miki would do.

Miki slowly looked up and turned to the girl. "I'm sorry. What?"

"You. You smell pregnant. Papa taught me what that was when I smelled that same scent on my aunt. You didn't smell like that last night. But you do now." The girl shrugged. "I guess you had a busy night." Then, after destroying his entire world, the little bitch left.

Miki turned around, but kept her head down, her hands flat on the stainless steel kitchen table. She began to tap both her forefingers against the metal and Conall watched all the wolves jump. Dunwich waved at him, trying to catch his attention. Then he mouthed something to him.

"What?" he mouthed back.

Dunwich held up his hand. Forefinger out. Thumb up. The other fingers bent into the palm. His hand looked just like a gun.

Oh, shit.

Conall glanced over at Miki and that's when he saw the gun in a holster and attached to her waistband. He didn't even notice her putting it on as they got dressed after their shower. Conridge must have let her keep one for the ride back.

And when Miki suddenly hit the table with her hands, every wolf but him and Van Holtz hit the floor.

Miki pushed her chair back. She looked at Conall. "I'm going to the bathroom. Then we are leaving."

"Miki, I—"

"No. There's nothing to say right now. And I mean *nothing*." Miki looked at Conridge. "Thank you for everything, Dr. Conridge."

"Anytime. Of course, when we take on a Clan of hyenas together, I'm pretty sure you can start calling me Irene."

"Thank you, Irene. I'll call you tomorrow about your job offer."

"That's fine."

She looked at Van Holtz. "Thank you for everything. I truly appreciate your hospitality."

Simply from the expression on the man's face, Conall got the feeling Van Holtz would be retelling this story until the end of time. "You are more than welcome."

Miki looked around the table and realized that all the wolves had disappeared. She leaned down and looked under the table. Twelve wolves laid out on the floor for no apparent reason—that didn't seem to distract her one bit. "I just wanted to thank all of you for helping us."

"You're welcome," one of the Van Holtz wolves was brave enough to say.

With that, Miki stood and walked out of the room.

Conall closed his eyes. Like his fever from the night before, he was pretty sure this would get worse before it got better.

Conridge leaned across the table and touched Conall's arm. "I wouldn't worry." She motioned toward her husband. "I stabbed him in the leg and set his Mercedes on fire before I agreed to marry him. She just needs time."

Conall frowned. "Uh...thank you?"

∽

Miki said nothing during the whole thirteen-hour trip that Conall and the Pack turned into a ten-hour trip by doing some seriously illegal speeding and keeping the bathroom and food breaks to a minimum. But really, what the fuck was she supposed to say?

The borrowed SUVs the Van Holtz Pack lent them pulled up in front of Sara and Zach's place. The Alpha pair already outside, since one of the Pack called ahead.

Miki got out of the vehicle. She was barefoot because she couldn't bring herself to wear Doc Martens boots with sweatpants. She wasn't a fashion maven, but that was too tacky for words. She limped slowly toward Sara, her calf tender but already healing. Her friend's eyes locked with hers and she pulled away from Zach. Sara knew something was wrong. The three friends always knew when something was seriously wrong with one of them without any of them having to say a single word.

As she reached Sara, Conall walked past her. He didn't speak, simply went into the house. Zach followed after him.

"Your leg?"

"It'll be fine."

Sara stared at her. "What the hell's going on?"

Miki glanced back at the Pack members behind her.

Sara motioned toward the house with her head. "Go."

And they did. Once they were gone, Sara turned back to her.

"Okay, dude. What's up?"

Miki looked at her oldest and dearest friend and burst into tears.

$$\mathcal{E}\mathcal{O}$$

Conall had just punched a hole in the wall when Zach walked in. He closed the door and stood behind him.

Leaning his head against the wall, Conall closed his eyes. "She's pregnant."

"I know. I could smell it a mile away."

"She won't stay here."

"She has to. Pregnant with a Pack baby? She'll have every Pride member in North America gunning for her ass. And who the fuck knows what's going on with that Clan. Besides, you marked her. She's yours."

"Not if she doesn't want to be. You know that as well as I do."

"Well, you can't go around hittin' walls. The house won't last."

$$\mathcal{E}\mathcal{O}$$

Miki sat at the kitchen table with her head resting on her arms, a glass of buttermilk sitting in front of her, and Sara's nose sniffing the back of her neck.

"What the fuck are you doing?"

"You smell different."

"According to Conridge's demon child, I'm pregnant. And the little bitch found 'flaws' in my thesis."

Sara pulled away, sitting down opposite from Miki. "I'm sorry. What?"

"You heard me. Flaws! In *my* thesis! Can you imagine?"

"I don't mean that, you idiot! I mean the...pregnancy?"

"Oh, yeah. That Cro-Magnon impregnated me."

"Did we not use the condoms Angie and I provided?"

"Yes, *we* did. But this happened during his fever."

"Where were you?"

"Half-asleep."

Sara smiled. "Was it good?"

"God, yes." Miki covered her head with her arms. "The man fucks like a god."

"Not everybody can be loved by Thor."

Miki lifted her head just enough to glare at her friend. "Shut up."

"So...am I happy or sad for you?"

"Christ, Sara, I don't know. I wasn't exactly planning on having a baby, you know, ever."

Sara suddenly became serious and Miki raised her head to look at her.

"You know, Mik, no matter what you decide, I'll stand behind you. Always."

Miki almost burst into tears again, and she never cried. But knowing that Sara would always be there for her meant more than she could ever say.

She wiped her eyes with the palms of her hands. "That means a lot to me. But I think...I think..."

"You want to keep it, don't you?"

"I'm an idiot, aren't I?"

"Why would you say that?"

"Because I'm going to end up like my mother. Alone. Struggling with a baby."

"Okay. First off, never ever worry about that. I've always got your back, Mik. And my potential niece or nephew will always be taken care of. *Always.* So that's not even an issue. And you know Angie feels the same way."

Miki wiped her eyes again. She really hoped she was pregnant; otherwise, she was becoming an emotional mess for no reason.

"And second, you'll never be alone. You've always got me. You've always got Angie. And you'll always have the Pack."

Miki snorted at that. "Are you kidding? They're only nice to me because of you."

"That's a load of shit." Sara stood up and grabbed a box of chocolate from off the counter behind her. "They like you."

"Yeah. Right."

Kelly and Julie pushed the glass doors open and walked in. They were both naked having, Miki assumed, just shifted. *If I'm going to stay, I guess I'll have to get used to this whole naked thing.*

Whoa! What the hell am I thinking?

"Hey, Mik. You're back."

"Yeah. I'm back."

"Well, me and Julie are hittin' an after-hours club tonight.

You should come. It'll be a blast. We'll celebrate you being all PhD and shit."

Miki laughed. "Thanks. I'll let you know."

"Cool." Kelly grabbed a handful of cookies from a bag off the counter while Julie grabbed two glasses and a gallon of milk. They disappeared through the kitchen door and then came back two seconds later.

Kelly sniffed the air. "Oh, my God! Who's pregnant?"

ॐ

Conall had his head buried under the covers, but Zach just wouldn't leave.

"I mean, how attached can you be to her?"

"I marked her and she's carrying my baby!" Conall barked from under his comforter.

"You breeders never fail to make me laugh."

"Just because you want to be childless—"

"Sara and I prefer child*free.*"

"You're an asshole, Sheridan."

"Yeah. I know. And she loves me anyway."

Conall brought his head up from under the covers. "And you love her?"

"More than anything."

"Why?"

Zach smiled. "Because she puts up with my shit without taking my crap."

"Miki calls me Viking."

"Well, she definitely has your number. All those other

bitches bought into your sweet act. That always drove me nuts. You always got more pussy than me."

"That could be 'cause you were always a sarcastic asshole. Next to you, I always seem like the nice one. Besides, I would do anything not to be like my family. Even be nice."

"You keep forgetting that *we* are your family. Not those crazed idiots. And we both know, I'd kick the shit out of you if you started acting like them."

Without knocking, nine of his Pack mates, all male, walked into his bedroom.

Mac Sumner leaned against the dresser. "So. You knocked her up, huh?"

With a growl, Conall pulled the comforter back over his head. Suddenly, he wished he were an orphan.

&

"Well, you have to think about this logically."

Miki didn't know when this became a town meeting of the Pack females, but before she realized it, twelve of them had joined the conversation. Five she'd never even met before. They all had opinions and they were all supportive. It was the wackiest thing she'd ever experienced. They treated her as if she were one of them and as if this problem were theirs to solve as much as it was hers.

"How logically? Either she loves him or she doesn't. Either she wants to stay with him or she doesn't." Kelly, thankfully now dressed, was short like her. But she was as feisty as a mini-Pinscher on six cups of espresso, and had a low voice like rough sandpaper.

"It's all so black and white for you," Patty snapped. "Maybe she doesn't think that way. You always forget that humans think differently."

"Bullshit. Miki's more wolf than a lot of us."

Miki looked over at Sara. She, too, was clearly enjoying the way this conversation was going. The women had already wrestled the box of chocolate from Sara and now all the females were partaking. Miki desperately resisted the urge to remind them that dogs shouldn't eat chocolate.

"Look," some chick named Mindy cut in. "This gets us nowhere. We should just ask her if she loves him."

They all turned to her.

Miki stared at them. She had just admitted this truth to herself. She wasn't sure she was ready to announce it to a room full of strangers.

Sara reached over and handed Miki a piece of chocolate. "It's got walnuts."

Miki took the chocolate and stared at it. "Thanks."

"You love him, don't you, Mik?"

With an anguished groan, Miki shoved the chocolate in her mouth and put her head back on the table.

"There's no shame in loving Thor." And she could hear the humor in Sara's voice. "He's the god of thunder."

ॐ

"I think we're avoiding the most important question here. What matters most. What means the most to men like us."

Conall growled at Billy Dunwich's sincere face. "I am *not* telling you if she swallows."

Dunwich smiled. "Just tell me if she's a good girl...or if

she's a *very* good girl?"

℣

Sara ended the call on her cell. "I left Angie a message. She'll probably call you later."

"She's only going to give me shit."

"That's her job. Mine is to be the supportive friend."

"Well, supportive friend, what the hell should I do?"

"How the hell should I know?"

"I knew it! You send me off into the desert then leave me alone to die. I should have never listened to you and Angelina. As soon as those fangs started coming out, I should have run for the hills."

Miki glanced up when the room fell silent. "What?"

"What do you mean his fangs came out?"

Damn. She really needed to watch what she said and when. Of course, that only took her twenty-nine years to discover.

She cleared her throat and shifted uncomfortably in her seat. "Sometimes his eyes would change and his fangs would come out."

Sara leaned forward. "During sex or when you pissed him off?"

She again glanced around the room filled with Pack females. They all seemed to be waiting for her answer. "Um...well, both. Sometimes."

Miki reared back when the chanting began. "Mi-ki! Mi-ki! Mi-ki!"

Now she was completely confused. "What? *What*?"

Sara jumped out of her chair. "Dude. You got the guy to

extend his fangs during sex. That's amazing!"

Kelly appeared equally impressed. "We're trained from preteen years to control that since a lot of us have relationships with humans without them ever knowing. We fuck 'em, but we don't necessarily mate with 'em. Anyway, it's really rare for us to, you know, 'bust out' during sex. Even with each other."

"So, if you actually got him to lose control that much..." Mindy shook her head.

"And this is Conall we're talking about. He doesn't lose it. Ever."

The females actually high-fived each other.

"Wait. Wait." Sara quieted them all down. "So, Mik. What about you?"

"What about me?"

Sara placed her hands flat against the wood table and raised an eyebrow. Miki had the feeling her friend was getting even with her for the rave comment from four days earlier. *Bitch.* "Was your reaction equally as *enthusiastic* as his seemed to be?"

Miki stared at the women, then buried her head back in her arms.

She heard Kelly's voice announce, "Ladies, I do believe we have a screamer."

Her cheeks were burning so bad she was sure they were about to burst into flame. "I hate all of you."

⁊〇

"She's a prime piece of ass, but once she pumps out a kid, that ass is going to go."

Conall glared at Jake. He wondered whether it would really be morally wrong to kill the man.

"I don't care." Conall moved his glare to Zach. He blamed him for this. "If it was only about her ass, trust me I would have fucked her and walked away by now."

"How could any wolf walk away?" That from Dunwich. "The woman took on a hyena Clan. She set them on *fire*. Personally, I'd rather have her on our side."

Zach shrugged. "Then it sounds to me like you love her. And if you love her, then tell her she belongs to you and she needs to get over it. Show her who's in charge. That's what I did with Sara."

Zach seemed less than pleased when they all laughed so hard Conall actually fell off the bed.

ॐ

Miki glanced up as Patty put a glass of milk in front of her. She stared at it in confusion because she hadn't asked for milk.

Patty shrugged and answered her unasked question. "Well, if you're going to keep it, I'm pretty sure you're supposed to drink milk and stuff."

"We'll have to get books. You know. On pregnancy and shit," Kelly suggested.

"And I'm in for the delivery room."

"Yeah. Me, too."

"Me, too."

Miki couldn't believe it. These women were volunteering to be in the delivery room with her. To help her without her even asking. So this was what it meant to be part of a Pack. She felt that sudden urge to cry again, but it disappeared as soon as the wolf females looked at Sara.

She knew what her best friend was going to say before it left her mouth. Miki wasn't wolf, but she could smell the panic and fear coming off the woman.

"You must be fuckin' kidding me! Sorry, Kendrick, you're on your own once that water breaks."

છ

"You know. This is bullshit." Conall didn't like the sound of that as Zach straightened up and headed for the door. "I'll tell her she's staying."

The males looked at each other then they charged after Zach. As Conall followed, he could see his future with Miki slipping through his hands.

છ

"And what about my career? Conridge offered me a teaching position."

Sara smirked. "First off. You hate teaching. You hate college kids. And second, Northern California has gotten really progressive and they actually have a few colleges. Some universities, too. This state is making quite a name for itself academically."

Miki gave Sara the finger as the females began laughing. But when Zach, Conall, and a group of Pack males walked in, all conversation stopped.

Zach looked at Sara. "What?"

Sara's eyes narrowed. "Just wondering what you want."

"What makes you think we want anything? This is my fuckin' kitchen, too."

"Uh-huh."

Zach went to the fridge, and tossed each of the men a beer. Once they each had one, he headed toward the swinging kitchen door, pushed it open, then stopped. "But if I were going to say anything—"

"*I knew it!*" Sara stood up. "You just can't stay out of it, can you?"

"Sara, wait." Miki stood up. "I wanna hear what the brain trust has to say."

Zach glared. "Look, Tinker Bell, I tolerate you 'cause I have to. But Conall, against *my* better judgment, loves your psychotic ass. I don't know why. I don't understand it. But he does. And I have to figure if he loves you, and Sara—who I trust with my life and the life of my Pack on a daily basis—loves you, then there must be something about you besides that big mouth and those tiny elf feet."

Miki's eyes narrowed as she crossed her arms in front of her chest.

Kelly leaned in between the two. "Why don't I just take this for now." She plucked the gun and its holster off Miki's sweats.

Conall sighed. He'd had some big plans for his life with Miki. House. Kids. Gun shows. But his best friend was blowing that all to hell and back.

But he'd forgotten about his Alpha Female. She was in Zach's face so fast that everyone, even Miki, stepped back.

"Was that supposed to be nice!"

"She doesn't get nice. She gets barely tolerated."

"You need to back the fuck off. *Now!*"

"All I'm saying is if she loves him she should just fuckin' stay!"

"And it's none of your business whether she loves him or not. Whether she stays or not."

"Sara, she's already part of the Pack. She protected Conall. You. And now she's carrying a Pack baby..."

Miki cut in then. "*Never* call our baby that again."

"...But if she doesn't want him for the love of all that's holy, put the poor guy out of his misery."

Conall could still hear them going at it, but he hadn't taken his eyes off Miki. He was waiting for her to realize what she'd just said. It took her all of thirty seconds. He knew the exact moment, too, by the look of pure panic on her face when she looked at him.

He smiled. A big, leering, Viking smile, he was sure. And Miki was none too happy.

"That meant nothing!" she practically screeched.

Sara and Zach snapped out of their argument as Conall moved in front of Miki.

"That meant everything, Miki-baby. Absolutely everything."

"You're fuckin' high. It was a slip. Nothing more. I haven't made up my mind about shit!"

The two stood toe-to-toe. But for once Conall didn't crouch down to meet her gaze.

"Just get over it. I love you. You love me. And we've got baby furniture to buy."

"You're not railroading me, Viking."

"You are so in love with me, you don't know what to do with yourself."

"You are delusional!"

"Marry me, Miki Kendrick."

"Not on your life!"

"We'll have a May wedding. Or September. After the baby or before?"

"I will kill you in your sleep."

"You'll try."

"You are making me crazy and I am sure that's not healthy for *the demon seed I'm carrying*!"

He smiled in the face of her yelling. "Is that any way to talk about our love child?"

Miki let out a strangled scream of pure frustration. And in response, Conall's smile just got bigger.

"That's it!" Miki barked. "Move the fuck out of my way!"

And everyone did. They watched as she stormed out, then they all looked at Conall. He was still smiling. He couldn't help himself. Miki made him smile.

Zach shook his head. "Are you sure you know what you're—"

Miki's voice slammed into them through the swinging door. *"Move your ass, Viking!"*

Conall looked at his best friend. "I do love that woman."

"They have treatments for that kind of mental disorder, ya know."

Miki stood in front of Conall's bed and gawked at it, marveling at how big it was. He must have had it specially made so that his big feet didn't hang over the edge.

She crossed her arms in front of her chest and braced her legs apart. *Big-footed bastard.*

He walked in and closed the door. He ambled over to her with that Viking grin plastered all over his face. "So whatcha want, baby?"

She gritted her teeth. Could he sound any more smug? "You're just lucky they took my gun."

He slid his arm around her waist and leaned down to whisper in her ear. "You wouldn't really hurt me, would ya?" He nipped her earlobe and a delicious bolt of heat ran down her entire body. "Wouldn't you rather fuck all night until we can't walk?"

His hand slid under her sweatpants and she pulled herself away from him, scrambling across the room. He took a step toward her and she held her hand out. "Stay!" He smiled at her. The most beautiful smile she'd ever seen. She loved him. She hated him. She couldn't imagine her life without him.

"I don't get you, Viking. Why are you so happy?"

"'Cause I love you, Mik." She warmed at his statement. "And because I won." Then she became hot.

Miki growled. "You did not win."

"I so won."

He wanted to play that game? Fine.

She smiled. "So you think you won?"

"I know I did. I love you. You love me. And I get to keep ya."

Miki nodded. "Did I ever tell you that the FBI has a corkboard with my picture on it? Actually, it has me, Amy, Craig, Kenny Liu, and Ben. And our pictures are in this pyramid shape, but I'm at the top. I heard the agents throw darts at it." His smile slipped a little. "The CIA still calls me every six months to ask me if I want to work at their...and I'm quoting...'labs'. They never get very specific, but you've seen the kind of stuff I can create so do the math. And there are several states in this country that I'm not really allowed in for...ya know...ever. And for the next forty or fifty years you'll be busy trying to stop me from saying something rude or inappropriate, or you'll be trying to stop someone from killing me because of something rude or inappropriate that I said that you didn't stop me from saying." She grinned. "So tell me, baby. What exactly did you win?"

Sure. He could have gone for a nice, normal girl. Or at least a girl who could shift into something other than human. But no, he had to fall in love with Miki Kendrick. Hacker. Scientist. Nut case. Great lay.

His mate.

The woman who would be driving him crazy for the rest of his natural-born life—if he were lucky. She smiled at him. And he realized she was as much a Viking as he was. No wonder she saw through his bullshit. Nope, he was getting just what he deserved. Who knew the gods liked him that much?

"Whatever. Let's fuck." He moved toward her and she backed away from him.

"First some ground rules."

He growled. "Such as?"

"I don't make breakfast. I don't clean. I don't involve myself in any clubs or associations that use the word mommy on their letterhead. At some point I'll actually know what I want to do career-wise which means the demon spawn I'm breeding will be pretty much yours to deal with until he or she is sixteen. By then they're ready for the SATs and that's when I step in. Now, of course I'll talk to him or her before then if I must. And no, this deal does not involve breast milk. I'll make sure to take care of that myself. Now, of course, this is all subject to change if their IQ is higher than 140. Then I'm on deck when they're five. After the baby is born, we can discuss marriage. But I'm not changing my name and the word obey will not be used in the ceremony."

"Is that it?"

She smiled. Yup. There it was. A big ol' Viking grin. "If I stay, I want a concealed weapons permit. And good luck with that since I'm sure all my federal friends will be fighting you tooth and nail on that one." Her smile softened. And it was a smile for him and him alone. "And I do love you, Viking. Just don't try and use it against me."

Yeah. He was definitely the luckiest man in the world. "Now are you done?"

"Yes."

"Good." He proceeded to untie his boots, tug them off, and toss them across the room. She watched him for a good while before she finally said anything.

"What are you doing?"

"Getting naked." He pulled his T-shirt over his head, then he moved to his jeans.

"Why?" She backed away from him, a smile threatening to spread across her beautiful face.

"So I can have my filthy, dirty, Viking way with you." He kicked his jeans away. "So I can keep everybody awake all night and show 'em how you're a screamer." He walked toward her, and she slammed up against the nightstand. "So I can make you come and come and come until you don't even remember your name."

"That's a hell of a plan." Cool. She was panting again. He loved when she did that.

"I like it." He stood in front of her. "Now here are *my* ground rules."

Miki tore her eyes away from his cock to look him in the eye, her arms again crossing in front of her chest. "Which are?"

"When we're in here. You're naked. I don't care if we're ninety. You're naked."

"I don't—"

"Did I argue during your ground rules? Quiet."

She fell silent, but not before growling.

"Back off Zach. He's the Alpha Male, my best friend, and my brother. So no telling him to go fetch unless he started it."

"But he—"

Conall covered her mouth with his hand. "Not. A. Word." She rolled her eyes and glared. "I expect you to always have two pairs of those pumps you had in Seattle. The heel is to be no less than five inches. One pair red and one pair black. They'll only be used in here. And you'll be naked. Also, I make the bed every morning, but feel free to sniff it whenever you feel the need. And don't get too attached to any of your clothes. Because if they're not off when we get in here, I'm ripping them off. And I really like ripping them off. Because I like you naked."

She pulled his hand away from her mouth. "Anything else, Viking?"

"Just one thing." He pulled her crossed arms apart and stepped into her body. He kissed her neck, her shoulder, her chin. Then he lifted her up. Automatically, her legs wrapped around his waist, her arms around his neck. She dug her hands into his hair and pushed her small body up against his. She stared into his eyes and smiled. A smile that was for him and him alone.

"No matter where we are. No matter where we go. Or where we end up. That you always...and I mean *always,* Miki Kendrick..." he leaned in close, "...make sure our freezer has cherry ice pops."

Miki burst out laughing as Conall carried her to their bed.

Epilogue

She forced her eyes open. Her head throbbed. Her back hurt. She felt pain in her arms and her knees. She sat up, slowly, and kept her eyes turned away from the French windows that had bright morning light streaming through them.

She waited until she felt like she could look around without throwing up, then she took in the room. It was beautiful. Gorgeous furnishings. Hardwood floor. Soft bed with a steel frame. This room alone must have cost a pretty penny to furnish. Gold silk sheets with a frighteningly high thread count covered her naked body.

The bedroom door stood open and she wondered whether she should make a run for it. She was pretty sure, though, that she'd start vomiting as soon as she stood up. But she wasn't too worried. Her wounds were dressed. Her body cleaned. The last thing she remembered was something, a lot of somethings, coming out of the trees by her store and charging her. They had resembled dogs almost, but she really didn't know. She remembered going for her gun, then something from behind...tackled her? And that was the last thing she remembered.

She rubbed her temples and tried to piece together the last few hours. That's when she heard it. It wasn't a growl. Or a roar.

It was a purr.

Angelina Santiago looked back at the bedroom door and watched a six-hundred-pound tiger walk by. It stopped. She could still see its tail swinging slowly from side to side. Then it backed up, turning its majestic head to look at her. And she looked at it. She patiently waited for the fear to set in. And the pure unadulterated panic that comes with it. Then it shifted and spoke.

"Well. Hello, sugar."

Angie let out a cross between a sigh and a breath. "Oh, shit..."

About the Author

To learn more about Shelly Laurenston, please visit www.shellylaurenston.com. Send an email to Shelly at shelly_laurenston@earthlink.net or join her Yahoo! group to join in the fun with other readers as well as Shelly. http://groups.yahoo.com/group/shellylaurenston

Is Emma ready for a bite?

The Wallflower
© 2008 Dana Marie Bell
A *Hunting Love* story
Halle Puma Series Book 1

Emma Carter has been in love with Max Cannon since high school, but he barely knew she existed. Now she runs her own unique curio shop, and she's finally come out her shell and into her own.

When Max returns to his small home town to take up his duties as the Halle Pride's Alpha, he finds that shy little Emma has grown up. That small spark of something he'd always felt around the teenager has blossomed into something more—his mate!

Taking her "out for a bite" ensures that the luscious Emma will be permanently his.

But Max's ex has plans of her own. Plans that don't include Emma being around to interfere. To keep her Alpha, Emma must prove to the Pride that she has what it takes to be Max's mate.

Available now in ebook from Samhain Publishing.
Available in the print anthology Hunting Love, *March 2009.*

Enjoy the following excerpt from The Wallflower...

She pulled the creamy, lacy shade down over the big picture window, effectively closing her in the twilight gloom of the shop. Becky had already rung out the register and was happily doing the accounts in the back, a pot of coffee and a huge container of Kung Pao chicken at her elbow while Emma finished closing down the front.

Emma loved this time of the evening. The streets were quiet, except for a few people heading either home or to their favorite restaurant for dinner. The soft light of early evening cast a glow over everything it touched, making it seem softer, more romantic. With a sigh, Emma headed into the back to gather up her coat and purse. With a wave to Becky, who waved her fork back with a grin, Emma slipped out of the back of the store.

"Emma."

Emma shrieked, staggering back and pulling her can of mace out of her pocket before realizing that the man standing in the shadows was Max. "God damn it, Max!"

"Sorry." He didn't sound all that sorry; he sounded like he was trying not to laugh. "Don't break out the grapefruit spoon just yet."

Her heart was still beating a mile a minute. She put the mace away and glared at him. "What?"

"Well, jeez, is that any way to greet someone who's here to help you?"

Putting her hand to her chest, Emma glared at him in the dim light. The son of a bitch was laughing at her. "Help me with what?"

"Getting Becky and Simon together, of course."

"Huh?" He looked entirely too smug as he moved closer to her.

"You want to get Simon and Becky together? I can help you with that." He picked up her arm and placed it through his, trapping her hand beneath his own. Suddenly he frowned and looked around. "Where is Becky, by the way?"

"She's still inside, working on the accounts," she answered absently, momentarily distracted by the feel of his arm under her own. It felt like it was hewn from rock, strong and solid and probably immovable.

His face blanked. "You came out here, at night, by yourself." It wasn't a question, it was a statement. He sounded like he couldn't quite believe his ears.

"Yeah. I do that every night. I'm parked right over there." She pointed with her free hand and gently tried to extract her other one from his suddenly iron grip. Becky lived in the apartment over the shop while Emma lived in an apartment in a complex on the other side of town. When Becky was done with the accounts, and her Chinese, she'd probably head upstairs to her tiny apartment and veg in front of her TV.

"You carry mace. I assume that means there's some crime in this area."

She nodded slowly. "There's crime everywhere, even here, what with the college nearby."

He was beginning to worry her. His face was still blank, but something about his eyes had changed. They glittered strangely, almost as if he were angry. She decided not to tell him why she carried the mace.

"Have you been attacked out here before?"

Emma winced and quickly tried to cover up the telltale sign

by babbling. "It's perfectly safe out here, and Becky keeps an ear out for the sound of my car. Any minute now she's going to run out here ready to annihilate anyone who's bothering me, so you might wanna let up on the death grip!" Her wince was now one of pain as his hand squeezed hers in a vice-like grip.

He let go and stared down at her. She could have sworn his eyes were gold in the moonlight before he blinked, the illusion fading back into his normal blue as he prowled around her, circling her like a predator. "Who hurt you, Emma?"

"What is wrong with you?" Emma took back her hand and rubbed it, wondering if she'd have a bruise. She glared up at him, waiting for an answer.

Max's frown was fierce. "I want to know who hurt you, Emma. I want to know now."

The note of command in his voice was one she'd never heard from anyone before. He compelled her to answer him in a primal way, forcing her body back against the brick wall of the shop with his own, looming over her in a way that both frightened and soothed her. Part of her wanted to bow down submissively and answer anything he asked of her. It took every ounce of her will to sniff and reply, "I have no idea what you're talking about."

She saw the shock on his face as she turned her head away, dismissing him. She ducked under his arm and started walking towards her car, her back stiff, her chin high. "You know, not every woman appreciates the caveman routine. Why don't you try it out on Livia? I'm sure she'd appreciate it!"

She gasped as her body was yanked back into the hardness of his. She could feel him in every atom, as if he was deliberately imprinting himself there. "If I'm reacting this way, how do you think Simon will react when he hears Becky's here alone?"

Emma gulped. Becky who? Involuntarily her hand came up and grasped the arm around her waist, her nails digging in with pleasure at the strength in it.

"Um, I don't know?" God, her brains were completely scrambled if that was the best she could do. "Hit her over the head with a club and drag her off by her hair? Not that he'd have all that far to go; she lives over the store, for God's sake."

He leaned down, his lips tickling her ear, his hair brushing hers, blending with hers. His other arm came around her waist, pulling her tighter into his body. She felt completely surrounded. She could feel his erection against her lower back, hot and hard as an iron bar, and gulped. "Why do you carry mace, Emma?"

"Why do you care, Max?" She tried to ignore the feel of his lips as he—

Did he just kiss my ear?

"Emma. Tell me what I want to know."

"And you'll go away?" She tried to ignore the incredible feeling of him gently rocking her in his arms. Yeah. That's it, I'm gonna start struggling any minute now. Any minute...

"Hell, no." He laughed gruffly. He put his chin on the top of her head and continued to rock her. When her stomach rumbled embarrassingly beneath his hands, he stilled. "Emma? Am I keeping you from your dinner?"

"At this point, you're keeping me from my dinner AND late night snack."

"Hmmm. In that case, I suggest we go out to eat. Maybe after I feed you you'll be more willing to tell me what I want to know." He sounded positively cheerful as he grabbed her hand, whirled her around and half dragged her towards his blue Durango.

"Gee, Captain Caveman, care to slow down? I didn't agree to go out to dinner with you."

He huffed out another laugh and opened the SUV's door. "In you go!" He gently lifted her into the seat. "Food. Then fight. Okay?" And with a smile he pushed her legs inside the SUV and shut the door.

She considered opening the door and hopping out, but part of her (okay, the majority of her) wanted to see what the hell Max was up to. Plus, hello! Dinner with Max! Could there be a downside to this?

She snapped on her seat belt as he got into the car. She hadn't enjoyed sparring with someone this much for a long time. "Don't think you're going to get what you want just because you buy me dinner."

"I wouldn't dream of it," Max purred, starting the SUV.

"Oh, boy," Emma muttered as Max, with another choked off laugh, drove out of the parking lot.

GET IT NOW

MyBookStoreAndMore.com

GREAT EBOOKS, GREAT DEALS . . . AND MORE!

Don't wait to run to the bookstore down the street, or
waste time shopping online at one of the "big boys." Now,
all your favorite Samhain authors are all in one place—at
MyBookStoreAndMore.com. Stop by today and discover
great deals on Samhain—and a whole lot more!

Samhain
Publishing Ltd

GREAT cheap fun

Discover eBooks!

THE FASTEST WAY TO GET THE HOTTEST NAMES

Get your favorite authors on your favorite reader, long before they're
out in print! Ebooks from Samhain go wherever you go, and work with
whatever you carry—Palm, PDF, Mobi, and more.